By Daniel L. Naden

A HellBound Books Publishing LLC Book
Houston TX

A HellBound Books LLC
Publication

Cover and art design by
HellBound Books Publishing LLC

www.hellboundbookspublishing.com

Printed in the United States of America

Acknowledgements

Getting a story across the finish line in the race from the writer's brain to the hands of the hopeful readers (or, perhaps, hopefully into the hands of the readers) is always a team effort. *Parting Shot* had a somewhat longer course to run than most, a sad story that really doesn't matter because it's relevant to me and boring to the rest of the world. Suffice to say, I had a lot of good help, getting *Parting Shot* to the end of the race. I'd like to thank a few, and apologize to the ones I forget to mention.

Special thanks go to Becky Narron, who is about the friendliest and most positive people you'd ever want to know. She gave me a hand with *Parting Shot* when I thought it might never find a home. I'd also like to thank James Longmore at HellBound Books for giving me a chance and believing in my story. Thanks to Alex Marroquin and James for suffering through punctuation hell and giving *Parting Shot* a well-needed polishing.

Finally, I'd like to thank my lovely wife, Paula, who has had to endure years of me obsessing about, or ignoring, my writing and has somehow managed to stick with me despite my quirks.

Other Books by Daniel L Naden

Drawn
Last Word
Picture the Flame
Silhouette
Stacked
Winter Breeze
Loss
Just One

Parting Shot

CHAPTER 1 -- THE YARD

The shoe was on the other foot.

But the foot had become detached and was currently holding the intense interest of the zombie near the shed. Another zombie, one with a rather significant overbite, had wormed his way through the abdominal wall and gotten himself a mouthful of intestines. The overbite, however, kept his teeth from cutting cleanly. Now he was hopelessly tangled in what could only be described as a gutsy web of shit. A different knot of zombies must have, in their living lives, heard the all the old leper jokes. Some were doing their deal-level best at trying for a face-off in the corner. Another unfortunate undead dude who lost his poker face was just about ready to throw in his hand. His heart was definitely in the game, but he simply couldn't keep his head on the task at hand, or the hand at task.

From the depths of the shadows cast by the eaves looming over the backyard deck, I'd watched the undead tuck into Stine where they'd cornered him against the fence. When the first of them pushed into the backyard,

I tried to hold him back to keep him from breaking cover. He heard them rattling up against the fence latch, heard the creak of the hinge as they forced their way through the gate, saw them shamble around the corner of the house, and just about shit himself. They got close to us, and Stine lunged away from me. I caught a fistful of his collar, but he twisted and shrugged out of it. Left me with nothing but the shirt off his back, literally, as he tore off across the yard.

I haven't the slightest idea in hell what he thought he was going to do. Maybe he figured he could bull through them at the gate and escape to the wide-open streets. But he knew, or should have known, that wide open doesn't exist anymore. There were just too many of these fuckers in the world. So, I dunno what happened. Stine was scared and just panicked, I guess. Maybe after all this time, it finally got to him. The running. The fighting. The hiding. The slow starvation. The loss of friends. The horror of watching the world die, one mouthful at a time.

He ran.

At first, it looked like he might get lucky and find a gap between the first group of three or four that were already in the yard, and whatever others might be following. His luck, however, wasn't luck at all. Stine rounded the corner and bounced off the chests of about ten more, all bunched up together in a clump. He turned with a squeak, like a terrified mouse, and ran right into the waiting arms of the first group.

"Poor soul," I whispered. "You were just too high strung."

I figured the folks who made the film: *Tombstone,* wouldn't mind me stealing one of Val Kilmer's famous Doc Holiday lines. Especially since all those movie people were either dead or eating.

"BRIAN!!!"

Stine had called to me, only that once, but never got to finish his train of thought. One of the taller zombies took a chunk out of his throat, ripping the voice box clean out of his neck. The rest pulled him to the ground.

To my reckoning, I exhibited a supreme amount of self-control. I could have thought of the requisite lump in the throat joke as the mob started working in earnest on Stine, but I knew I wouldn't be able to hold out on the bad jokes forever.

Stine was going, going, gone, pretty much like everyone else.

I felt nothing, but I knew that proprieties must be observed. Even from a quiet man on a quiet Earth. And so, my running commentary, my coping mechanism, took over. A twisted smile in the face of madness. Laughing at the terrifying.

The undead thronged to get their bit of what was possibly the next-to-last-guy in this part of the country, perhaps even the world. There was a shitload of them in the yard now. They'd formed a circle around the Stine-shaped buffet bar, with the ones in front kneeling, while the others were practically climbing over their backs to get some of the good stuff. They looked like a retarded rugby scrum. I half expected Stine's liver or stomach to go squirting out across the lawn, pounced upon by some undead bastard, only to have the scrum re-form again on top of him.

I almost laughed aloud at the imagery. Rugby with Stine's liver. Soccer with his balls. I suppose they were gonna bowl with his head, too.

It was funny.

One of the zombies stepped away from the pile with a handful of skin or muscle or something. Most of its abdomen was gone, and I could see its spinal column through the hole. It jammed the wad into its mouth and swallowed it whole, like a dog gulping raw hamburger, but the food fell right out of the rib cage and onto the ground where the fucker proceeded to pick it up and try the whole thing over.

Hilarious.

You can't buy comedy like this, especially these days. The giggles hit me and I fought them hard, trying like hell to keep quiet and stay still. I was seriously in danger of laughing myself right the fuck to death.

Still, the habit of self-preservation is a hard one to break. I closed my eyes and focused on breathing slowly until the giggles left me, one muffled hiccup at a time.

None of the zombies had noticed me yet. They couldn't see me and I must've been downwind and . . . well . . . I had gotten pretty good at standing perfectly still. Ten years, with six or seven billion undead on the planet, you figure out how not to be seen, heard, or smelled. Right now, though, I was on the clock and it was really just a matter of time before they found me. In a way, that clock has been running since the zombies took over the world: it's always been a matter of time.

***

After a while, the zombies finally finished up with Stine. Usually, when the dead are done eating, they just lose interest. That's what they did here. Almost as if on cue, they stopped pressing in around his body and quit squabbling over the various pieces of him scattered around the yard. They didn't leave, though. They just began to mill about, like a candy store flash mob a couple minutes short of 'go'. A bunch of undead, hanging around without a care in the world, but always ready in a perfect position to flash or mob at just the right time. Like the time when someone loses their nerve, panics, and invites himself to dinner. Or the time when someone has a giggle fit in the shadows.

In my expert opinion, that's the worst thing about the undead: they don't do anything. At least, they don't do anything unless it involves eating. So, when there's nothing to eat, they just stand there, wherever they happened to be. Kinda like middle schoolers at their first dance, hanging around and hoping someone else will be brave enough to get things started. The bad part is that, unlike middle schoolers, the undead aren't shy about following the leader. So, if one finds you on the dance floor, so to speak, the rest will go all mosh pit on your ass in a heartbeat. No wallflowers when it comes to undead dining.

In my case, the zombies milling about left me in a bit of a spot.

I was safe for the moment, a wallflower tucked into my friendly corner of nowhere: dark, unseen, or unsmelled. Eventually, though, I'd have to move. I can stand still for a long time, but not forever, and this back yard was short on exits. Just ask Stine, or at least what's left of him. The only gate in the entire perimeter of the six-foot privacy fence was guarded by a healthy horde of zombies who were still picking Stine out of their teeth. Now they had an entire eternity of hanging out with me to keep them busy. Waiting for me to start the dance, I guess.

I was gonna have to leave sometime. The question *du jour* was how.

CHAPTER 2 -- THE SHACK

There's a trick to finding a good hiding place in a zombie-filled, post-apocalyptic world. In general, zombies slowly trudge along after what they see. While their memory is unsurprisingly thin, the draw of fresh, living meat seems to stick with them when little else does. So, if they see you heading in a certain direction, they'll follow. If you duck into a house or building, they'll follow you there, surround the place, and congregate around the doors. Then, you're pretty much fucked. Starve to death or fight your way out, neither choice is optimal. What's worse is that some of the undead seem to hang onto a random bit of intelligence. They don't really remember things, but they *do* problem-solve fairly well, especially when food is involved.

Stine and I had been hiding, living here in the backyard, for a couple weeks. We came here, as usual, on the run from undead unfriendlies, after being shaken out of the old shack that had been our previous bolthole. We'd been on kind of a bad streak, losing a couple temporary homes, one after another. Ordinarily, if we had picked a solid spot, we could get to stick around awhile before we were forced to move again.

We selected this backyard on the hoof, as they say. It probably wasn't the best five-star-quality hiding place that Stine and I could have found, but it wasn't the worst place we'd ever stayed either.

Our problem this time was . . . well . . . time. A fellow can outrun the undead hordes because, quite simply, they're not built for speed. Then again, they don't really need it: they've got numbers, and they've got all the time in the world.

***

Lesson *du jour*, folks . . .

Wait.

Did I really just use *du jour* again? God, my vocabulary skills are going right the fuck down the toilet. These days, I find myself stuck on a single word or phrase, using it over-and-over like a broken record until somebody smacks me upside the head to skip me outta my rut. Since my good buddy Stine is no longer up for the job, I'll have to try harder to mix things up.

So, lesson of the day: when you're trying to ditch a mob of the undead, you have to be careful. Run too fast and you leave them behind. They'll eventually forget about you, sure, but they're still hanging around whatever area they found you in, so you can't go back. Run too far away, and you get to parts of the city you haven't scoped out very well. No man's land, or more likely, dead man's land. You could find, for instance, the entire population of the Macy's Turkey Day parade, all undead and filling up every square inch of every street and sidewalk for several square blocks. That's a good way to end up being dinner for an entire undead marching band. Maybe, instead, you find a subway full of zombie commuters, or a day care full of honest-to-God ankle biters.

You get the picture: if you don't know the terrain, you're probably fucked.

Ultimately, when you gotta run from the deaders, you're wanting to lead them off for a while so the mob gets enough momentum moving away from wherever it is you don't want them to be, then keep going. Might take months for them to eventually wander back once you've given them the slip, maybe if you're cautious and lucky.

That's the theory, anyway. *Brian's Rules for Zombie Mob Manipulation.* Number one with a bullet on the New York Times Bestseller list. The rules work pretty well. Usually.

Unfortunately, the mob that attacked our shack caught us off-guard. They hit us at night, and because we were so fucking sure that we were safe, they hit us when we weren't keeping watch. They hit us — and every single one of us was asleep.

***

Our shack had been a perfect spot. Tucked into the Bottoms — an abandoned industrial area just west of downtown — the shack and the area around it were remote enough in the *before* time. In the *after* time, there just wasn't much in the way of interesting food to attract the undead hordes. Better still, the shack sat in the middle of an empty lot, without any decent lines of sight from the roadway overhead. I think the lot used to hold a factory or warehouse way back when, but the building had burned or collapsed of old age and was eventually razed to the ground.

The only structure that remained was that dilapidated old shack.

It was square, about ten or twelve feet on a side, and looked like it had been pieced together with scraps. A slanted corrugated tin roof sided with rotting plywood and a heavy door that latched with a rusted hasp and a bent-nail pin. I honestly couldn't tell if it had been constructed as squatter's lean-to, or if it had been some kind of a lame utility shed that survived the destruction of the factory.

Coming in on the run, like we'd been at the time, it had been a pretty good safe house for us. We could slip in and out of the Bottoms, could hang out and move around without having to look over our shoulders every second. Better still, with about fifty yards of empty lot surrounding us, we could see shit coming long before we were wiped out (if you get my meaning).

Of course, we didn't see the shit coming for us because, like I said, we were tucked in for the night.

We'd been there for a few days, arriving on the heels of having to leave quickly when one of our temporary hideouts had been overrun. We'd been on the lookout for a new, more permanent spot for us to settle down, and had narrowed our options down to a couple of finalists. Unfortunately, neither place worked out, so we ~~had to move again and~~ ultimately ended up at the shack as our go-to spot.

A couple days at the shack came and went with no problems. We started settling in. Earlier that afternoon, we'd raided one of our many supply caches to stock up on eats and stuff, so we were going to be good for a few days. We ate, joked around a little bit, and with dark coming on, turned in for the night.

Inside the shack, we'd blacked out the windows so we could have lights on after dark without drawing unwanted attention. Carson had wedged his pallet against the door, the bulk of his hulking Hulk of a body serving better than a deadbolt or padlock. Sharon and Davies tucked together, spooning under a blanket in the corner. They were kind of a long-running couple. Stine was sprawled in the middle of the floor. For a tiny guy, he could take up a ton of room. Allie had stretched out along a wall, right underneath the window, with her head in a corner. I chose to copy her, but on an adjacent wall, so that our heads were close enough for us to talk. We'd talked well into the night before we drifted off. The last thing I remember before I fell asleep was listening to her soft, steady breathing. I heard a grunt from near the door, and I thought Carson might've still been awake, but he might've just been starting to snore. It was hard to tell. Eventually, sleep caught me. Warm and cozy with people I saw not just as survival buddies, but real friends. Family, really, if such a thing existed anymore.

I woke to the sound of wood cracking — a weird kind of fucked up alarm clock — and then a chunk of wall fell over on top of me. Undead poured through the walls, like the doors of a loaded subway car coming open. Bodies, hands, and teeth fell on us. The sounds that followed . . . God almighty . . . utter carnage.

Chaos.

Screams, undead, and feet stepping on me and on everyone else; the stink of corpses and sound of flesh tearing and the shrieks of my friends dying while more and more zombies piled in. It was like a bad orgy scene, except the zombies were the only ones getting it on. My friends were getting it off, so to speak. Skin. Guts. Whatever.

I was blind lucky to escape. I still don't know how I survived. Maybe I was close enough to the wall that it hid me when it fell and left me covered enough to avoid notice. I lay still for what seemed like forever — it might've been a couple minutes, might've been a year — with what felt like an entire marching band walking across the slab of plywood that lay across my stomach, the fulcrum on the world's most fucked-up teeter totter. The dead couldn't stand still while they were standing on me, so they kept piling into the shack. Eventually, I figured out that I needed to get out, somehow.

Inching at first, I slipped out from under the plywood and took a quick look. The zombies were thronged in a clump around where Carson was, or what remained of him. Another clump was in the corner where Sharon and Davies had been. Fortune was on my side as the zombies standing over me were focused on the crowds they could see. Carson. Sharon. Davies. The only zombies that could see me, a meal still alive and uneaten, were on the others side of the shack. I decided it was time to make a hasty retreat.

Clawing through walls of bodies, grasping arms, stench, and vitriol so bad it almost took me down all on its own, I fought my way through the dead assholes moshing through the shack. I figured they overlooked me as I escaped because they were too intent on the feeding frenzy —then they face-palmed later (I suppose) as their rotted little minds realized a meal had slipped away.

It wasn't until I broke through them that I saw Stine pushing through the crowd on the other side. We both started sprinting, dodging stragglers. We stopped to catch our wind after a few blocks. We had gained some distance on the deaders who decided to come after us, so it was (mostly) safe enough to pause.

Bent over, hands on my knees and gasping, I asked him, "Anyone else make it out?"

He shook his head.

"I didn't see anyone else get out. I can't imagine that they did," he said.

"All dead, then?"

"All dead. Every last one."

"Allie, too?"

"*All* of them!"

We were quiet for a few seconds, watching the numbers of our pursuers start to swell.

"What now?" I asked.

"What do you think, idiot?"

He was right. What else could we do?

We ran.

***

We lost everyone at the shack: Sharon, Davies, Carson, and Allie, all gone as quick as you can say midnight snack. We used to be the Six Musketeers. After the disaster at the shack, we were down to two. Just Stine and me. Our group went from a couple of Three Musketeers to a freakin' Twix bar. Which is pretty disturbing just thinking about it.

Now, watching Stine bite it — or vice versa, I guess — there's just me. Call me Snickers.

God, I really am cracking up, aren't I?

***

In the end, we should've known.

We all knew about the dangers of hiding inside a single, undefended building, and committing ourselves to the illusion of safety that comes from having four walls around us. We should've known. Even after everything that's happened to the world, we let ourselves get suckered in. Sometimes, the idea of shutting out the mess that the world has become . . . well . . . it's just too tempting to resist. Out of sight, out of mind and all that.

Who knows? Maybe when all this zombie shit started, *inside* would've been okay. While the ranks of the undead were still relatively thin and there were still plenty of people left behind who could fight and defend a place. While there was enough food and water left to be stockpiled. While there was enough of the world — enough hope — left to make holding out and playing 'Alamo' seem worthwhile.

I'll tell you, though — there's something shortsighted about hanging onto hope in an end-of-the-world like ours. To put it simply, for every safe hidey-hole that held a handful of people steadfastly determined to ride out the storm, there were millions, *billions*, of people in the world who weren't hidden and safe. People who, instead, ended up as lunch or partial lunch for the Earth's new overlords. Or underlords. Or undead lords.

Whatever.

That kind of hope ignores the semantics of getting access to clean water, the dumping of piss and shit somewhere far enough away that it doesn't stink up the place, or the need to forage for food. It glosses over cooking your food, all the smoke and smell. The need for clean clothes, or fuel to run generators, keep the place warm, and run electronics.

Basically, the hopeful vision of hiding from a zombie apocalypse is shit. You gotta go outside sometime. No matter how careful you are, going out and about will eventually draw the wrong kind of attention; and with a world full of the hungry bastards hosting our apocalypse, drawing attention means drawing crowds of those undead fuckers. Crowds of zombies hanging around your hidey-hole means that, once you're in, you're in for the duration. However long it takes you to starve.

Or, however long it takes them to find a way in.

CHAPTER 3 -- THE YARD

In the yard, from my vantage point on the deck, I watch an undead zombie-chick stumble. Kind of a stupid thing for her to do, really. She hadn't even been walking, *per se*, just shuffling her feet and distantly gnawing on something that looked vaguely like one of Stine's fingers. Suddenly, she catches a toe in the turf and almost goes down in a heap.

Like I said before . . . pure comedic gold.

Her almost-pratfall is enough to snap me out of my reverie. She's gotten pretty close while I was daydreaming. Close enough to get my attention. Close enough to make me nervous.

I give her a once over, trying to figure out if she's going to come up and join me on the deck. In the light, I can't be sure, but she kinda looks like Sharon from our group. Could it be?

Mentally, I give myself a little kick.

It's not really her. Of course, it's not. She couldn't have turned zombie and shuffled here, just in time to eat Stine. Besides, Sharon probably didn't fare then much better than Stine did. There wouldn't have been much of her left to turn. Not with the mob that had been dining on her in the ruins of the shack.

You wanna know a big occupational hazard of being a post-apocalyptic survivor in a world full of zombies? It's too easy to see people you used to know in the faces of the undead. Maybe it's like all those folks who used to see Elvis or the face of Jesus on a pepperoni pizza. Or a Rorschach test, except it's old pals instead of ink blots. In a way, it's like being haunted by six billion ghosts: all those folks who died while you live on.

It has its way of sneaking up on a guy.

Sharon or not, because the zombie chick is eating, she's still moving. The somnambulism of most the other revenants had wound down to the point where they were mostly standing still, zoned out. Waiting for something to move. Waiting for the next thing to eat.

The Sharon-thing's tangled feet take a moment to untangle. She stumbles again and looks for sure like she's headed to the turf. Some odd remnant of motor sensory skill keeps her from falling onto her face, but her antics seem to catch the others' attention and agitate them a bit.

They all start shuffling again, random motion and random speeds, like the world's worst game of freeze tag — but where they all get to move, and I have to stay frozen the whole time. Just like that, the amount of time I could stay hidden here in the shadows gets a helluva lot shorter.

***

My thoughts keep circling back to the shack.

We lost everyone else there. Did I mention that already? Sharon, Davies, Carson, and Allie. Now I've lost Stine. As the last little piggy, will I go wee, wee, wee, all the way home?

We'd been close as our little group. Sounds kinda sappy for me to say it like that, but we were. Almost like family. Which is to say, we *were* family. It's just a label that's hard to cling to, what with the world being like it is.

Standing here, stuck here, I close my eyes and I can imagine big, bad Carson crushing his way through the throng in the yard, bellowing like a bull, coming to save me. I can almost see the light glinting off Sharon's sniper rifle on the roof of the house across the way, ready to start *pffftin*g the ones who get close to me. I can see Davies and Stine, gutting zombies with longswords, crushing them with truncheons, and laughing it up as they joked their way to me. I can hear Allie, whispering in my ear.

I can imagine they're all coming to save me. But they're not. They're gone.

While I'm here.

Alone.

CHAPTER 4 -- THE END OF THE WORLD AS WE KNOW IT

The world ended quickly.

It took only three months from the time the very first outbreaks of zombies started popping up on YouTube until the time that the governments and armies of the world collapsed, leaving the rest of us to survive on our own. You can imagine the anarchy that followed was pretty brutal.

Three months. In that brief, chaotic time, two-thirds of the world's population either died or were turned into zombies. More realistically, two-thirds died *and* were turned into zombies. When it all first happened, there just weren't enough of the undead to swarm and fully chow down on everyone who died. Not nearly enough to give 'em the ol' Stine treatment and devour the bodies completely. Those concentrations didn't come until later.

After that first three months, half the world's survivors died in the three months that followed. War, famine, murder, and flat-out crazy brutality. The undead were bad, to be sure, but when it comes to true nastiness, nothing can beat the ghastly creativity that we humans inflict on each other, even when our own survival hangs in the balance.

That time of chaos, death, murder, and war? I survived the way that most people survived: pure luck. The day the undead exploded across my city, I had ditched classes with a glorious hangover. Mom and Dad went to work. My younger sibs, Mark and Emma, were at school. So, I sat alone, watching TV as the metro fell apart. If I'd gone to class, I would've died on campus when the buildings disgorged their diligent, class-attending students onto the commons to eat everyone else. I'd have died like my family and most of the people in the world. Instead, I survived, crying at home with my hangover while they were featured entrees on the all-you-can-eat humanity buffet. Some luck, huh?

I didn't learn much those first few weeks, other than to keep my head down and to keep away from everyone. The zombie bug spreads fast. If you get bitten, you're dead in an hour. Then you're back up and biting not long after that. Hang around someone who's been bitten and you can catch it from the air coming out of their lungs — or from the odd bodily fluid you might pick up during that hourglass span of time between bitten and turned. At that point, the hourglass flips and the sand starts falling for you, too.

At the start of it all, most of the infected dead hadn't started rotting yet, so they looked fairly normal — right up until the time that they're chewing on you. Most of the living, yet infected folks just seemed like they had bad allergies, so the initial infections spread through entire populations in an impressively short span of time. College campuses. Office buildings. Schools. Homes.

Nasty stuff.

By the time the news coverage started showing zombies ripping people apart in the street, it was far too late. People were turning too fast to quarantine or kill, but *just* slow enough to make sure that they spread the disease around while they were still alive.

In its wake, civilization did a Hindenburg-like, slow-motion crash into the ground.

At first, panicked survivors across the world looked to their governments to save them. Laughable, I know, thinking that institutions created to maintain order — to maintain civilization — would somehow be adept at handling civilization's collapse into chaos and anarchy. But hey, we humans are social animals. We crave social order. It's only natural that folks looked first at the social order they were most familiar with. Of course, the governments were gone, just as overrun and overwhelmed as everyone else. As were the religions, families, *et cetera, ad nauseum*.

It's ironic, though. Our instinctive drive toward social order worked against us in dealing with an epidemic of zombies and the ready ways their infection could spread.

While there were still more survivors than there were undead, folks flocked to the safe zones and shelters. Of course, those places were perfect breeding grounds for more disease. Even the best-secured perimeter couldn't help an airborne toxin spreading among row after row of frightened refugees. The government camps went down almost as quickly as they were set up.

As did the governments themselves, falling one by one in a silent film, Keystone Cops-style montage of futility.

The remnants of the world's militaries took a crack at addressing the problem. When I tell you that there were some truly epic battles, you should understand that I mean the militaries dropped some serious shit on the undead. As I understand it, the entire continent of Africa will be glowing for however long the half-life of forever calculates up to be. Unfortunately, dropping entire arsenals of nukes didn't really turn out to be the panacea they thought it would be: nobody wants to be eaten by a radioactive zombie.

In most places, though, the military waged a bunch of land battles. A million little skirmishes fought worldwide against billions of undead. Not good odds, but worse considering that there's just not enough ordnance to keep you from being overrun or, worse, decimated from within your own ranks.

When the military failed, I fully expected the world to devolve into some kind of *Lord of the Flies* rehash, where strong-arm groups would form and draw, or collect, members to them. But I was wrong.

The strong-arm groups: the soldier wannabes, the socialists, the churches, the cults, and the slavers all lined up in their respective fiefdoms like the cheesy gangs from the old movie, *The Warriors*.

All of them fell apart. Every last one.

What took their place? Nothing. Not much, at least. The whole idea of society fell apart with 'em. Whenever people tried to form up some group or society — anytime they tried to carve out a place for themselves — they would attract the undead. More and more, all drawn to the hustle and bustle of folks trying to live together, in whatever form that took. Or, they would catch the disease and make their own zombies.

For a couple years, you could hardly find more than a couple people to rub together, or whatever that saying used to be. Folks just holed up on their own, too afraid of getting sick or eaten to do much socializing. At least, that's how it was in my city.

I'm pretty sure it was the same all over.

***

Eventually, though, people started to organize together again. What can I say? We're social animals, after all.

We were ultimately saved by the deaths or zombification of almost every human on the planet. I guess that, once you die and become a zombie, you quit breathing and the virus or bug or whatever it is can no longer go airborne. Sure, you can still get sick by the more mundane methods of being chomped on, or in an ill-advised exchange of bodily fluids, but catching the bug from the air became less of a factor as the surviving population density dropped to Ice Age levels.

More to the point, after five years or so, the billions of zombies that were left were getting pretty hungry. So, the odds of someone actually surviving a zombie attack long enough to become a kind of airborne Typhoid Mary weren't very good. Usually, the zombie mobs don't leave much behind.

So, new groups started springing up again. Family-sized groups small enough to avoid notice, and agile enough to move quickly. Most kept to themselves, although I heard that cults and slavers had a mild resurgence during this time.

I was alone for a lot of that period.

I just couldn't make it work out. I never could find the right bunch of folks to hang with. Which is, I suppose, my way of saying that I sucked at getting people to like me or appreciate me. I drifted in and out of a lot of different groups. Sometimes they asked me to leave. Sometimes I left on my own. Sometimes, I just had to escape because . . . well . . . sometimes, people are assholes.

Slowly, as time wore on, I began to despair ever finding people again; of being around others and belonging. But then, one day, I accidentally stumbled into a group. A handful of decent people and good survivors. The group with Carson, Sharon, Davies, Stine, and later, Allie.

CHAPTER 5 -- PEOPLE

I came across Carson looting the cafeteria kitchen of a comfortably abandoned office complex. This many years since the world ended, food could be tricky to find. So, figuring out where to collect food stores was a bit of an art form — one, that I learned later, Carson excelled at.

Most of the obvious places had long been cleaned out. I mean, the stores? Those were wiped out in the first week or two. Took a couple years for folks to work out that restaurants would've had tons of canned or dried goods, and then to get all of them picked over. Most people just aren't smart enough to think it through. After the end of the world, the notion that restaurants might have food supplies beyond what they might get from the drive-thru window would baffle a lot of people. Go figure.

It was longer still before survivors had cleaned out food banks, shipping warehouses, and similar places. It was funny, in a way. For a while, people would fight and kill each other over finding some new source from the dwindling food supply. They'd kill each other and die, and the zombies would come and kill more or make the best of food supply locations unusable. Luckily, I suppose, evolution favors those bright enough to seek survival without pissing into their own bathwater because, eventually, there weren't enough people left to worry much about having to fight over the last of the prepared, preserved food.

I'd been watching Carson for a few hours. He caught my attention by moving furtively — the dead don't do furtive — as he slipped from building to building through the overgrown green space surrounding a long-abandoned office park. At the time, all I saw in him was just some freaky-big black dude, Michael Clarke Duncan big. I didn't learn his name until later. I crept right up on him after he went into one of the buildings through a broken plate glass window. At least, that's what I thought as I followed him stealthily through the window. Instead, I found his knife stuck up under my jaw.

"Whatchoo doin' sneakin' up on a guy?" he hissed in my ear.

"Sneaking*?*" I asked.

For some reason, my mind flashed to the scene with Gollum from *Lord of the Rings*, but I didn't know if the guy with the knife had a sense of humor, or was even a book lover. Or a Tolkien lover for that matter. So instead, I said, "Just seeing if you could use a hand. Y'know . . . doing . . . whatever it is you're gonna do."

He looked at me for a long time, quiet-like. Later, after I got to know him, he was a pretty normal guy. He was always calm, always reserved, and when he looked at you, you just *knew* he could fuck you up. He was just waiting for you to step into it . . . whatever *it* was . . . so he could calmly shift from his quiet, calm persona to quietly and calmly tear you apart. Did I say he was intimidating to a skinny white-guy with a big mouth and, apparently, not much stalking ability?

The dude gave me *that* look and, after an hour or so — or maybe just a few seconds — he kinda gave a little exasperated huff.

"Sneaking," he muttered, shaking his head.

Then he turned with a little grin on his face and went on into the building. I followed him in. It was dark inside. Hell, most places these days were dark. Not really the kind of place you want to be exploring when something hungry might pop out of the shadows and take a hunk out of your arm; the guy didn't seem to care much. He twisted through hallways and a maze of dark cubicles that made my nuts wanna crawl right back up into my gut, occasionally shining a little penlight to keep his bearings to wherever the fuck he thought he was taking us.

Before long, we ended up in a room with an all-glass interior wall that let out onto an enclosed courtyard. The sun was up high overhead, so we had a little natural light that cast the room in a thin gray shadow. All around us was a jumble of tables and chairs, some still upright, some tangled together (must've been a lunchroom). I saw a few bodies scattered throughout the area, but they weren't moving, even with the not-so-quiet entry we made. I figured they were dead and when I edged a bit toward the nearest of them, I could see shattered skulls ringed with dark circles of blood gone black with age. Gunshots at the centers of their foreheads so they'd stay down.

We did a short circuit of the room, looking for trouble, but finding none. The room seemed as secure as could be expected — I thought so and it seemed that the big guy did, too. He led me through a stainless-steel swinging door and we stepped into the kitchen.

One thing you gotta understand about the apocalypse, it *stinks*.

Kill off over six billion and, even if they're reanimated, they're still rotting. You gotta remember that dead folks aren't the only smelly things out there. Anywhere you might find food that's still remotely edible, you'll find the stench of awful food that didn't quite make it, even years and years after the power went out. Sometimes, it'd take a while for containers to fail and expose food to the air. Bags, cans, freezers. Wait long enough, and even the best-preserved canned goods would go septic and split out with high toxicity. Seals on refrigerators would fail. Walls on walk-in freezers would decay from the inside out. Ten years later, and food is still rotting. In the end, there's one unalterable truth: that shit smells bad.

By the time the big guy and I walked into the kitchen, the stench made my eyes water. The room smelled like the ass-end of a Romero walker with a bad case of '*braaaainnnns*' diarrhea.

Of course, by that time, we survivors usually didn't notice bad smelling stuff. Personally, I couldn't even begin to rely on my nose to scent an incipient zombie attack. After so long, I didn't usually notice their smell anymore. Maybe I've gone nose blind, like the odor spray commercials used to say all the time. The kitchen smelled a different kind of bad than undead bad. The kind of bad I actually could smell with *my* nose. Awful, but it was worth tolerating, because what Carson had found was a smelly kitchen: one that hadn't been looted yet.

We stopped a few steps inside the door and began the methodical process of searching the place. We didn't find much in the cooking area, or around the cleaning area. In the back, though, we found a walk-in pantry as big as my parent's old basement. We glanced at each other with big shit-eating grins on our faces. The pantry was stocked floor-to-ceiling with goodies. A crap-ton of pasta that had somehow avoided plunder from mice and rats. Half the place was full of canned food and most of them were still unsplit and unspoiled. There was enough food here to last the two of us a year, maybe. Longer for me alone.

Or for him alone.

I stopped dancing for a moment. Yes, I'd been doing my version of a little jig — in my mind, at least — when the thought occurred to me that this was the big guy's find. He might not want to share. After all, sometimes, people are assholes.

He was giving me that look like he'd just read my mind while waiting for me to ask the question that would give him permission to calmly snap my neck with those big mitts of his. The thought occurred to me again that here was one scary dude.

Fortunately (for me), his face broke out into a grin. I swear it was like someone turned on the fluorescent overhead.

"Too much shit here for me to carry out on my own," he told me. "Got some other folks coming in a bit, but we could use some help. That is, if you're willing."

I had an idea, a sudden brainstorm . . . but I paused and acted like I was thinking about it. Not for long — maybe, less than a second.

"Sure!" I said. "But . . . um . . . you got a place to keep all this stuff? Other than here or where you're staying?"

His smile clouded over a bit. I could see the thought taking hold, a seed of doubt I was trying to plant. I always was good at seeing flaws in everyone else's plans.

"Damn," he said. "I didn't think that far ahead. You don't think this place is good enough?"

Hell, I didn't *really* want to piss on the guy's parade, but by this time, I'd been around the block a time or two. I'd seen a lot of what did and didn't work in our brave, shitty world. If there was one thing that I did know, it was not to put all my eggs in one rotting, hard-to-get-to basket.

"Might be okay," I said slowly, "leaving the food here."

I let the moment hang a bit.

"Problem is this place is a death trap. Dead fuckers see a bunch of folks coming in and out all the time, you could end up trapped in here. All the food in the world in this building, and instead of eating it, you get eaten."

"Shit," he said. "Got any bright ideas, smart guy?'

Once again, I made a show of thinking it over. The fuck of it all was that it took the end of the world for me to find out I would've been a good car salesman. After the pause, I pinged as if I had just gotten hit over the head with the glittering wand of the idea fairy.

"The biggest deal with all this is that the food's all in one place," I said. "If this place gets overrun, you lose the lot of it. If it gets raided by someone else, you lose the lot of it. Or you go to some stupid war turf, trying to save it from them."

I paused again, this time, purely for dramatic effect.

"What if we were to split it up, put chunks of the food into a bunch of different places? Maybe store only enough for a couple weeks in any one place so if we had to, we could hole up and be able to stay out of sight for a while, if we had to, and not starve right away while we're waiting for things to clear up."

He scratched his chin. I was almost certain he was doing it purely for dramatic effect.

"Pretty smart," he said.

For that briefest of moments, I thought I had him sold. I was starting up on that mental happy-dance again. Then, he spoke up.

"You got any bright ideas, then, about how we gonna get all this food to all those places without drawing every zombie this side of the Mississippi to us? Or those turf-war guys you said we might have to fight? Or how we gonna even find all those good hiding places?"

I smiled and gave him an aw-shucks shrug of my shoulders.

"Maybe we'll have to make more than one trip?" I said. "But I know of a few hiding places we can try out."

"That," he replied, "is a good place for us to start."

"Good for me, too," I told him. "You think the food's safe in here while we're getting organized?"

"Sure," he said. "Nobody but you is dumb enough to try following me." He gave me his look again. "Or *crossing* me."

I must've looked a bit pale because his face split into another smile.

"Just shittin' you, man. By the way, Carson's the name."

I smiled back. "I'm Brian."

"Brain?" he asked.

I couldn't help it. I snorted out a laugh and said, "Yeah, whatever. Tell me one I haven't heard before."

Together, we slipped back out of the building and went looking for his friends.

***

Carson took me to meet the rest of his group. Sharon, Davies, and Stine, he named them.

They all were staying at a lovely little residential cottage, surrounded by a nice, white picket fence. The homey effect was wasted, though, because the yard was about two feet overgrown in grass and weeds. I guess they didn't bother to mow. Given the fact that lawnmower sounds would likely bring hungry undead things, I didn't blame them.

Inside, the cottage looked almost normal. That is to say, pre-apocalypse normal. A living room full of average-looking furniture. Along the front wall was an overstuffed couch that looked almost new. In opposite corners sat an armchair and a recliner. Both were showing some wear, as if the cottage's original inhabitants had favored them over the other furniture. Mom and Pop chairs I guess, with no Mom and Pop to sit while watching TV anymore. Beyond the living room was a dining room with an even more average-looking table and chairs. Somewhere at the back of the house, I figured I could find a classic kitchen. All of it was very ordinary. All of it, very normal. In a way, normal was nice. Not much pre-apocalypse anything left anymore.

Of course, the naked guy sprawled on the couch kinda broke the image.

Post-apocalypse, most folks weren't shy. Modesty ends up being somewhat *passé* with so few people left, but walking into a house and seeing someone with his dick hanging out is still a shock. Maybe it's instinctive or something. Maybe the Neanderthal versions of us started covering up our dicks because, when some 'Grog' you met had his dick out, it meant someone was about to get fucked.

Either way, I have to say that seeing the guy and his schlong was a bit of a jolt.

Naked Dude hopped up off the couch, scratching his junk with his hand, which he then stuck out, as if he expected me to shake it. His hand, not his junk.

"Stine," he said.

I cast a wary glance at the hand, then back up to his face.

"Like the beer mug?" I asked.

"Funny. Never heard that before," he replied. "Stine. Like *Stine*."

He looked over my shoulder at Carson.

"Hey, big guy!" Stuck the same hand out to Carson, who raised an eyebrow back at him then slowly flashed that smile of his. Stine pulled his hand back in a hurry. I promised myself right then and there that I'd learn how to do Carson's freaky, intimidating smile if it killed me.

"Okay, Stine," a woman said, coming down the stairs. She was carrying a sniper rifle with a scope that could've told me my DNA profile. Following her was a thin, balding guy.

"I'm Sharon," she said while shaking my hand. "That's Davies. And you are?"

"I'm Brian," I said. Then, struck by some kind of goofy stupidity, I added, "I followed Carson home. Can you keep me?"

Sharon shot me a look and I got the feeling she didn't joke around much. Then Davies shot me a look and I got the feeling *he* didn't like people joking around with Sharon, much.

"Um. . ." I said. I gestured at Carson. "This dude found a *huge* food stash and asked me to help him move it."

"That's right," Carson said, saving me from further awkwardness. "A whole cafeteria pantry, most of it canned or dry goods."

"Food?" Stine asked. He strolled over to stand in front of me and began to caress my cheek with, of course *that* hand. "Why the fuck didn't you say so in the first place, darling?"

He put on such a goofy-serious face, I couldn't help but laugh. Hell, I even heard a chuckle from Carson.

"So, hiding a buffet line someplace?" Stine continued, waggling an eye at Carson. "Where's the grub? C'mon, spit it out, man!"

"Uh-uh," Carson said. "Not until you get some clothes on. And wash up! I've seen where that hand has been."

We all laughed it up a bit. Tension that I barely realized was there slowly evaporated. Then we started to plan what to do with that cache of food.

***

In the end, we came up with a pretty good plan.

Among the five of us, we picked out seven or eight solid possibilities of places where we could store food without too much worry of it getting stolen, or attracting too much undead attention. It sounds easy to just say it, as if it all was gonna happen just because we talked about it, but we actually had to do logistical shit to get it all worked out. Just like a freakin' UPS ad. Took us a couple weeks to get the food all parceled out, but somewhere along the way, we kinda . . . came together.

Damn, but that sounds like some shitty *Kumbayah* moment. Back to sappy, sure, but it's what happened. To this day, I don't know if we really did connect like we were long lost quintuplets separated at birth, or maybe we just all needed to see new faces. More of the human race, the survivors. I missed people. Maybe they did, too.

Over the next few months, we worked well together. More than that, we fit well together, too. Each of us brought in different personalities and different, useful skills. Carson was good at exploring and finding food. He was also freaking huge, so if we needed muscle, he was a good guy to have around. Sharon was frighteningly adept at using that high-powered rifle. With the scope and muzzle suppressor, she could pick off zombies or other unpleasant folk from several blocks away without anyone being the wiser as to where she was. Davies and Sharon were a couple — at least, as much as you can be a couple these days. He was kinda quiet, but a genius with electricity, and a dead aim with a bow. Stine was a wildcard: brash, fearless, and about as arrogant a dude as I have ever known. Back in the old world, I'm betting he had ADHD, but I'm also betting he wasn't taking Ritalin for it, unless it was just for the high. The guy just didn't have a reverse gear. Everything went forward with him. In a lot of situations, a guy like Stine was invaluable because he just wouldn't back down from anyone or anything. Except, maybe, Carson.

I was the comedian, I guess. Too much TV as a child or something, but I shot my mouth off way more than the others. You could call it a lack of inhibition, since *all the world's a stage* added up to a world-wide non-zombie audience numbering in the hundreds — locally, in maybe the tens. I quit having to worry about stage fright or getting the bum's rush out of the place for telling bad jokes and worse puns.

I was also the planner. I'd been lucky surviving alone as long as I did, but I was also good at seeing what did and didn't work and how the people around me could best fit into place in my schemes and ideas.

We worked well together, right from the very start. For a while, it was almost fun.

Reality kinda sucks, though, when it jumps feet-first, into your life.

CHAPTER 6 -- LOST AND FOUND

We lost the house first.

It started one day with a zombie who showed up at the picket fence, looking for a way in for a quick meal. We'd been there for a few months and found it convenient because the cottage had plenty of room for all of us. We'd really started to settle in, and down a bit.

Somewhere along the line, though, we caught the attention of The Lone Deranger: that single undead fucker who had enough brainpower left to notice even the little activity we let show at the house and hung onto the notion long enough to find his way into ruining our curb appeal. The zombie showed up at the gate and Sharon put a silenced sniper round through his skull. We hoped that would be enough.

The next day, though, four zombies showed up. We took turns plinking them off — Davies embarrassed all of us with his archery prowess — but did so while the rest of us were packing our shit to leave the house for somewhere else.

We kept a watch that night, and at dawn, Stine woke us up to tell us that a mob had showed up. We left the house, left all the zombies at the front gate, and slipped away out the back. Whatever radar those fuckers were using to zero in on us, they'd marked that house. We'd never be able to stay there again.

We went to my old place next, but it was a real shithole by contrast: a convenience store I was staying in before I met Carson and everyone else. I liked it because of the view — I could see anything coming at me through the front glass. In retrospect, it probably wasn't my brightest idea, even for living by myself. Sticking the five of us in there was an even worse idea. A horde showed up, and this time, they showed up *en masse*, crashing straight through the glass. We were lucky enough to be able to fight our way through the wall of grasping bodies, or else we would've been done then and there.

To escape, we ran a pre-planned route with a lot of zig-zags so we could turn off and lose the pursuing mob. Escape routes were another one of my ideas. It's hard to run for your life and away from a throng of zombies without having an idea of where you're headed. So, I made sure we knew, and practiced, our escapes, hedging against the eventuality of needing a quick exit. When the mob finally lost track of us — or maybe, simply got bored and left us — I circled us back to a cache we'd set up inside a storage unit garage. We huddled in the sweltering unit, with the door cracked a bit, and caught our breath.

"Where to now?" asked Stine.

We all looked at each other. Nobody wanted to say anything, so I piped up.

"Y'know . . . living in one permanent place? It's not working out for us very well."

Sharon gave me a look, and then said, "Well, we weren't having problems before you showed up at our door."

Davies gave me his own look — this one a bit sympathetic — but said nothing. Carson and Stine became suddenly interested in their shoelaces. For a moment, just a single moment, my smart mouth almost got the better of me. Instead, I took a breath and told them all what I'd been thinking for the past few weeks.

"You're right, Sharon. A blunt bitch, but right. Whenever we've been living alone, we don't attract enough attention from *them* . . ." I waved an arm out beyond the door. ". . . to get them interested in us. But the more people we add to any one place, the greater the chance that someone gets seen. That someone gets remembered."

Sharon was still throwing the evil eye my way, but she was listening — and not pointing her rifle at me — so I continued.

"You'd think it'd be better, living alone or in smaller groups. That doing so would be safer. Maybe it would be. But I think it's kind of an illusion. A confirmation bias, if we wanna look at it scientifically. While we're living alone and not getting eaten, we think we're bucking the odds. But are we? If you live alone and somehow die, who's going to know it? If you live in a group and the group gets attacked, the survivors remember the attack and everyone who died and become nervous about living in groups."

Stine looked up from a candy box he was raiding. He pointed a Butterfinger bar at me and said, "Okay, gotcha so far. So, what's your point?"

"My point," I said, "is that maybe people *can* live longer together than we can alone. More hands, more brains, more eyeballs to watch each other's backs."

"Yeah," Carson said. "But it seems like we been getting our asses kicked for quite a while, now."

"Carson ain't lyin'," Davies said.

"The problem isn't the number of people," I told them. "It's staying in one place long enough to become a dinner bell."

They all paused for a moment. Sharon and Davies, I think, seemed surprised like the thought hadn't occurred to them. Stine looked indifferent, like he pretty much always did. He'd done a pretty good number on that Butterfinger, even though most of the chocolate coating had melted over his fingers and face. Carson looked the least surprised. He sat back in the shadows and didn't say anything, but he caught my eye and I thought he gave me an almost-imperceptible nod.

"You have a plan, then?" Davies asked.

"You betcha," I said. "Start plotting out places where we can all live, but plot them in bulk. One after the other.

"Meaning precisely, what?" Carson asked. I think he already knew the answer, but I appreciated the help, connecting the dots for the others, as it were. I returned his subtle nod.

"Start with places that are either well-defended or have open lines of sight. Make sure they always have an escape route we never use until we're done with the place."

"And then?" Sharon asked.

"And then, we set up shop. Stay there for a few weeks . . . or as long as it takes for the space to become unsafe."

"At which point, we move to the next," Carson said.

"Yep," I said, "That's my thought. My plan. Maybe not such a good idea, but things have been good, this time we've been hanging out together. Carson found enough food to keep us all from starving for a while and is a big, mean motherfucker. Sharon and Davies are good shots and are super-cute to watch, holding hands and everything. Stine? He keeps us on our toes . . ."

Stine tried to throw his Butterfinger wrapper at me, but it stuck on his fingers. He flipped me off, instead.

"We work good together. We're a good group, and I think we'd do better together than we would, being picked off, one at a time."

I paused to let 'em soak for a few seconds.

"So whaddya think?"

I don't know what I was waiting for. Maybe a big group hug, or maybe they'd all just say, "Fuck off, Brian", and toss me out on my ass. Instead, Carson stood up, walked over to the door and pulled it open. We all followed him out. Where else were we gonna go?

Somehow, in a world where conventional wisdom had people living apart and alone, we found each other and were successfully living as a group. Dare I say it again? As a family.

We lived like that for four years.

CHAPTER 7 -- THE YARD

In the back yard, standing on the deck, I get a bit of a respite from the zombie-chick that looks like Sharon. The chunk of whatever she's been gnawing on slips out of her hand and the zombies that have been migrating in her general direction, and in mine, all go down in a heap, grabbing for the meat on instinct alone. The Sharon-zombie gets an almost Sharon-esque look of exasperation on her face as she watches them. She doesn't dive into the undead heap with the rest of 'em, but neither does she keep walking my way. She stays put, so I have a little more time.

I watch the Sharon-thing standing impatiently without a clue as to what she's impatient about, and I can't help but think about our group. All these years, watching so many people die, you'd think losing a few more wouldn't be a big deal to me.

This group was different. Different to me.

I led our group to their deaths. I was the planner. They all listened to me. Hell, I was still looking at pieces of Stine littered all over the yard. So, yes, even an ice-cold bastard like myself is still feeling bad. Safe to say, my mood sucks, *really* sucks.

We had this thing we did when people died. We made jokes about it. *Really* bad jokes. A cold-blooded thing to do, maybe, but it made us feel better. Well, at least we feel *less* like cold bastards and more like humans. More like we were living, regardless of how bad things got.

Allie taught us that.

Of everyone in our group, I was always kinda sweet on Allie. She was . . . well . . . *different* from the rest of us. Full of life, which is a pretty fucking stupid analogy to use given what had happened to the world, but with her it was true. She had a way of looking at things that seemed, at once, upbeat and sarcastic. As if all the shit that had been happening around us, and to us, never really affected her. We learned just how significant that was. The tale of how she got to us was pretty awful, pretty infuriating when she told us. Allie had been forced to live through some really bad shit, but somehow, it didn't change how she went through the world; how she lived, day-in and day-out.

So, it's not surprising to find that I'm standing here, looking at something that looks like Sharon, who had been chewing on the last parts of Stine and yet the person I'm thinking about through all of this is Allie.

CHAPTER 8 -- ALLIE

Eventually, we moved into the outdoor lumberyard section of a hardware store.

We'd jumped around quite a bit since that day in the storage unit — maybe five or six different places over the course of three years, maybe more. Following the plan I'd laid out for us so many years before, we'd stayed safe, but I had the feeling folks were getting tired of being urban vagabonds. So, by the time we found the hardware store, I think we were all kind of ready to settle down.

The hardware store itself was an old Sutherlands that had half-burned years before. God only knows how it caught. Maybe it was burned in rioting, hit by lightning, or maybe set alight by some group of squatters at some point. I was always surprised how the main building of a lumberyard could catch fire and burn down while the big fucking piles of dried wood in the yard out back remained untouched. With no fire crews to put it out, you'd think the whole place would've burned to the ground. Maybe the wind was blowing away from the lumber that day. Either way, we were lucky.

Surrounded by wrought-iron fencing, the yard featured several hutch-like buildings where Sutherlands kept most of their wood. While wrought iron isn't all that good for obscuring the views of the nearby undead, the buildings were laid out in a staggered pattern that blocked the sight lines into the entire central area completely from the outside world. That gave us a lot of space to chill inside and out without being seen. Best of all, it was far enough off the beaten path where the worst of the hordes were located that we could make noise without drawing unwanted company. I mean, sure, we couldn't hold a rave or a group orgy or anything, but we *could* hang out. Catch some rays and stuff. After so many years of spending most of the time hiding inside, finding a place with our own 'courtyard' was pretty cool.

So, we set up a cozy little home. Almost a compound.

We made sure the sturdy gate in the perimeter fence was chained shut and impassable. A buffer area between us and the fence served as our no-man's-land. Anything strolling around in there was either an ejector-seat-warning that we needed to get the hell outta Dodge, a target for archery, or two-by-four batting practice (depending on the circumstances, of course).

We built our sleeping area in a loft where the lumberyard kept their smaller-sized boards. I grumbled a bit that we could find ourselves stuck up there if the zombies ever got past the fence — an argument I might've even won — until Sharon kicked out the vent screen from one of the gables in the roof and pointed out that we could give ourselves escape routes. We spent the next couple of weeks quietly plotting. Cutting doors and hatches that would let us slip quietly to the roof and, with a little luck, extend planks between the different buildings to give ourselves a path to freedom. It still made me nervous as hell. After all, we'd spent a long time living *on the hoof*, so to speak and hadn't been eaten yet. I wasn't entirely comfortable with breaking what had been a successful way of living for us just to set down roots, but they all had listened to my plan of constant mobility and they'd followed it for a long fucking time. Everyone was tired of moving around and sleeping in shitholes. I was tired of it.

Eventually, I gave in. *What the hell*, I thought. *It's worth a shot.*

Once we had the escape hatches done, we went a little crazy. Built beds and chairs. Built a pantry shelf to stack the food we wanted to keep on hand. We even rigged up a water collection system with plastic hose and big plastic trash barrels on the roof to catch the rain. Brought in mattresses from nearby abandoned houses and ran electricity from a generator we had running in a storm sewer. Took about a mile of heavy gauge wire we'd found in spools at yet another (unburned) hardware store plus way too many extension cords, but we put the generator deep enough that the horde couldn't quite figure out how to find the sound. It drew quite a crowd of 'em, but they gave up looking and took to standing aimlessly over a manhole cover a few blocks away. Eventually, I think they sort of got used to the sound. Who knew zombies developed selective hearing?

By the time we were done, we had a fairly primo setup. Not the Taj Mahal or anything, but it was comfortable, and pretty safe.

This is the point of my story where I'd like to say that we all lived happily ever after. Like the *Boxcar Children*, only in a lumberyard. Of course, Henry, Jessie, Violet and the other Boxcar kiddos never had to worry about being mobbed and ripped to shreds by the undead.

Nor did they have to worry about asshole slavers with a grudge.

***

We'd been at the lumberyard for quite a while. I don't really remember how long, but it was probably close to a year. Long enough for us to settle into a really solid routine. Long enough for us to get comfortable, not just with our place or the routine. We were comfortable with each other. I mean, I can't speak definitively for the others, but I know that I had never been as at ease in different groups as I was with these folks. I talk about family, but these people were closer for me. Maybe interpersonal relationships become easier when there aren't that many people left in the world, but it felt like we'd come together. If that doesn't sound too goofy.

That said, I could also tell that we were . . . wearing down.

One of the hardest things about surviving beyond the end of the world was futility. Yeah, it's difficult to get by when billions of zombies all see you as *hors d'oerves*. Harder still, when safe food and water and supplies and homes are in short supply and growing shorter every year.

What was *really* hard, though, was the sense that it just didn't fucking matter. Our group was very good at surviving, but what did we really have to live for? I mean, even with a lot of luck, was it reasonable to imagine we could live out the bulk of our natural lives? Could we really do another forty years like this, with the world dead and the survivors trudging along against unimaginable odds, year after year after year? Hell, another five might be too much.

For myself, I wasn't optimistic about staying alive another year. I was . . . tired. Just too tired. I didn't notice it as much while we were moving from place to place so often, but once we settled into the lumberyard, I realized just how dark my long view of the future had become. From that perspective, life was beginning to seem pointless.

So, it was that one bizarre day. We had just returned from a foraging trip and shuffled up the steps to our lumberyard loft to find a woman completely naked, sprawled out across Stine's bed.

She sat there, bold as hell, posed up like some freaking movie star, or porn star given her lack of attire. I couldn't help but think of the similarity to how I first met Stine. Of course, unlike Stine and his junk, this gal was gorgeous. Dark hair cut down to her shoulders and hanging halfway across her face. Dark, steady eyes, the kind that swallow you whole, and an epic body, of course. A body featured into every adolescent wet dream I ever had. Great body, yes, but I kept getting lost in her face, in those eyes.

Wow.

She looked at us leisurely and said, "Who's a girl gotta fuck to get a meal around here?"

***

As non-sequiturs go, it was a doozy.

Davies stood there; his mouth dropped like he'd been going to say something and just forgot. At his side, Sharon took it all in — the nude chick and Davies' reaction to her — and her face darkened as her eyes lit up with smoldering irritation. Carson said nothing — no big shock there — but his eyebrows arched so high that they were in danger of disappearing into his close-cropped hair. Which, after living with the guy for the past few years, was as surprised a response as you'd ever be likely to get from him. Someone else might've jumped out the window shrieking like a little girl or stood there with their eyes popping out of their heads like some Toon who'd just seen Jessica Rabbit. Not Carson, he just raised those eyebrows. He always was one cool cat.

I, on the other hand, was my usual smooth self.

"Umm . . ." I said.

Dumbass.

Stine saved us all from looking like complete doofs. Instead, he made us look like assholes. He walked over to the bed and unbuckled his belt.

"Me," he said, flashing her his least-sincere smile — the one that car salesmen or sleazy casting-couch directors used right before they bent over their 'victims', proverbially or otherwise. He stepped up to the woman.

Carson chose that moment to chime in. His voice was soft, but it carried weight.

"Stine."

I didn't think Stine heard him (Carson's voice was so quiet), but he did. Stine paused for a heartbeat or two, twitched just a bit, and then looked back over his shoulder.

"What, man? What's so important?"

The woman's move was so quick that I don't think anyone but me saw her draw the handgun out from under the pillow. She was pointing it at Stine's junk. Give the lady credit, she didn't just start blasting away. She just sat there, smiling a smile that put Stine's to shame. A shark had nothing on her. To this day, it still kinda freaks me out, just picturing it in my head.

"Dude," Carson told him in that same soft voice. "I don't think the lady was really offering."

Somehow, I found my wits to say something to her.

"Um, so I don't think you'll have to fuck anyone today, lady, unless you really, *really* wanna," I said.

The woman turned those dark eyes toward me and inclined her head without moving her gun even a fraction of an inch from bulls-eying Stine's junk. At the same time, Sharon's rifle materialized out of nowhere. I didn't even see the motion until Sharon had it on her shoulder with the barrel trained on the lady.

"You could probably go a ways better toward getting that meal, *chick,* if you told us a story," Sharon said, her voice frosty. "Like how you ended up, here, in our home. And whether or not you're bringing trouble our way."

"And why you're naked," added Davies.

Sharon's frosty-cold eyes shifted to a lava-hot glare, pointed at Davies. He shut his mouth with an audible click.

"But maybe we could lend you something to wear first?" Carson asked.

Always a gentleman, that one.

"Unless you really, *really* don't wanna," I said.

She just smiled at us, each in turn — a genuine smile this time.

"Name's Allie. And since you offered, clothing's always nice," she said flipping the safety on her gun and setting it beside her on the bed, giving it a loving pat. "Unless someone really feels inclined to come and play..."

Did I say that I liked Allie from the very start?

***

Sharon dug up a t-shirt and pair of shorts for Allie while Carson went to get her something to eat. Somehow, wearing clothes made Allie look as sexy to me as she did without clothes. That was funny, in a way. I'd been a little bit androgynous for a while. I hadn't had many sexual thoughts lately . . . none for myself and none for my friends. Part of that whole, despairing-of-living thing I'd been fighting, I think, so my reaction to Allie caught me by surprise.

Something about her set me off. I guess it wasn't just me, given Stine's reaction, Davies' awkward attentiveness, Sharon's cold jealousy, or even Carson's quiet chivalry. Allie affected us all. We didn't figure out right away whether or not that effect was a good thing or a bad thing, but hey . . . she'd gotten our attention and curiosity, I suppose. I knew I was definitely having trouble focusing on things, like what she was doing here.

Carson came back and handed Allie an old jar of black olives and a bag of beef jerky, so Sharon didn't waste any more time. She leaned in toward Allie, taking an interrogator's posture: all chill and down-to-business.

"So . . . who are you?" Sharon asked. Our self-appointed inquisitor, I guess. "Where are you from and why are you here?"

For a second or two, Allie looked at Sharon, a quirk of a grin on her face, the perfect counterpart to Sharon's scowl. Another standoff moment, perhaps. Like the one with Stine.

This time Allie shrugged, and said, "If you hadn't guessed, I'm on the run."

"From?" Sharon asked.

"Slavers."

"Ouch," Stine said.

Ironically, Sharon's hardass face softened, softer than I had ever seen in her. "Why don't you tell us about it?"

***

Slavers. God, I hate them.

Bad enough, the fucked-up part of human nature that makes people want to own and abuse others. Far worse, in my book, that we'd be this far into the end of the world and there would *still* be some of those kinds of assholes around. You'd think evolution would've kicked in before now.

Carson came up and put a big hand on Allie's shoulder.

"You were a slaver's captive?" he asked, quietly.

"Y-yes," she said. The tremble in her voice betrayed the first crack in the calm facade she'd showed us so far, as if Carson's kindness broke through her resolve. "I got out today and came here to warn you."

"Warn us?" Sharon said.

"Yes. The slavers have been watching you here. They're gonna come for you."

CHAPTER 9 -- SLAVERS

We all kinda picked our jaws off the floor. Stine recovered first. "Slavers? You brought slavers here?"

"No!" said Allie. "I said they were *already* watching you!"

"Yeah, right," Stine glared at her and glanced at her gun.

"Stine." Carson stepped in. "We should probably hear her out. Let her talk."

Stine held up his hands and took a step back, but his eyes stayed on her gun.

"Go ahead, Allie," Carson said.

So, Allie told us her story.

"For a while after the world went to hell," she said, "I lived on my own, on the fringes of wherever survivors gathered, but out of sight where I didn't have to worry about them, or vice versa. I got to be pretty good at hiding from all the chaos, and filching food from groups. At surviving. Like everyone else."

"Eventually, I ended up finding a bunch of people to stay with. Good people. Lived on the other side of downtown in an old parking garage we'd converted, kinda like you did with this place. They'd done their homework. They used parked cars and chain link fencing panels to create a perimeter for their compound to close off the ground level of the garage, so they were pretty safe from even a large crush of the undead. A couple levels up, they built a living area with framed-in walls and filled with furniture. They even rigged up a big plastic tank that acted like a water tower, complete with a rainwater reclamation system. We didn't use it for showers very often, but at least we could have 'em.

"All in all, it was a sweet gig. When I started out with them, I was quiet, reserved. Kept to myself out of habit, I suppose. I was just so used to being alone, but they were cool with me. They waited me out and eventually, I started to feel like I belonged there. I started to feel human again.

"I'd been with them for, maybe, six years when the slavers found us.

"I'd just returned with one of the scouting parties, hunting for supplies and food. We were the last group to come in and we'd been pretty lucky. Found a prepper's bunker with a bunch of MRE's and bottled water. We were all feeling pretty good — laughing, joking around. Good times.

"When one of the lookouts sent a warning signal, we all kinda shrugged it off. False alarm. Most of our alarms were false, after all. The signal system we used was simple: ropes running down from the top of the garage, tied to cowbells in the living area. If we heard one, it was usually that someone tripped over one of the ropes or was bored and wanted company. So, we thought it wasn't real. Then a second lookout sent a signal from the opposite corner of the garage roof, followed by the rest of the bells. All of them. All at once.

"We looked at each other for a moment — frozen with just a hint of the fear we were beginning to feel in ourselves. That fear reflected back in the eyes of our group, our people, my friends. Then we ran.

"Of course, we had practiced. We drilled every week on what to do if we were being overrun by the deaders. First and foremost, we had to make sure the fences were still in place: all the gates closed and reinforced. Our defenses were good, but they wouldn't help us at all if a bunch of zombies wandered in through a fallen fence or open gate. So, everyone split up, most of us sprinting to make a quick round of the perimeter. I ran up the stairs to the top of the garage to find out what the watchers had seen. They were all together, all four of them — Michael, Jenna, Susan, and George — leaning out over the top railing. What I saw when I joined them, I wish I hadn't. A horde of maybe two thousand undead swarmed in around the entrance to the garage. The middle half piled up against the outer gate; the other sides split around us like the tide, sweeping around a pier. Even from above, the stench was awful.

"Then the screams started. My people were screaming.

"I thought at the time that the front gate had been closed, in our rush to get our supplies into the living area, maybe we forgot to push a car back up against it. Without a car supporting it, the chain link alone was no match for the weight of the corpses, piling up on it. However it happened, the fence *had* to have collapsed. I could tell by the direction of the screams and gunshots coming from below that the gate was gone and undead were pouring into the garage. The five of us on the roof ran to the stairwells. We had to hurry if we wanted to save the others, to help them fight their way to higher levels and our escape ladder..."

Allie's shoulders slumped and she paused for a second.

"We were too late," she said.

"By the time we hit the stairs, we could hear the sounds of savagery. I'm sure you've all heard it before. The sound zombies make when they're eating people. That's what we heard, from the levels below us. We pushed as far down the steps as we could, but all we could see was a solid wall of undead, cutting us off, surging toward us. Maybe there were survivors down there, but we knew we weren't going to be able to save them.

We retreated back up the stairs to the roof and threw a bar across the door. Together, the five of us tossed the escape ladder over the wall. We'd made the rope ladder as a last-chance escape route. Rope ladders aren't very much fun to climb up, less so climbing down; since we'd picked a multi-level garage, we always thought the spiraling inclines would slow down whatever horde that might've breached a gate somewhere and give us a chance of climbing down and away from whatever was coming. Unfortunately, we didn't plan on being so completely overrun by so many undead. We didn't count on being caught so off-guard. Now we could hear shuffling steps echoing up the stairwell, working toward us around the ramps. They were close enough where we could smell their rot. We needed to leave in a hurry.

"George went first, legs up over the wall, and disappeared down the ladder with agility that belied his size. Jenna and Susan went next, Susan so close behind Jenna she was almost on top of her. Michael gestured for me to go.

I laughed at him and said, "Really? You're gonna play chauvinist on me now? Go, Michael!"

So, he disappeared over the rail. The first of the zombies had just appeared on the final ramp leading to my level when I went over the wall. I was halfway down when the gunshots started."

Allie stopped for a moment and took a swig of water. I think I was the only one of us close enough to see her hand shake, ever so faintly. She took a deep breath and continued.

"You see, they planned it all. The slavers. They knew us. Knew our defenses. Knew our escape plans. They somehow found a large horde and got it to follow them to our home. Led the whole lot of 'em right to us. If I had to guess, I'd say the slavers sabotaged the fences so the horde could get in that much easier.

"They were also waiting for us to come down the ladder, the slavers. They knew our ladder would drop us into an area that was reasonably protected from a horde. Then, they hid there until we were all stuck, hanging dozens of feet off the ground. All the better to pick us off, one-by-one, until they got the one they wanted. Until they got me.

"They shot George first because he was closer to the bottom, and because he would've been harder to stop once his feet hit the ground. Head shot. He probably didn't know what hit him. I think they might've saved Jenna and Susan to be slaves, but Susan lost her grip on the ladder, turning to try to see who was shooting. When she fell, she took Jenna with her. They landed in a pile, maybe thirty feet straight down from where they'd been on the ladder. I only took a quick peek at them. They looked broken. Neither was moving much.

"That left just Michael and me. I was above Michael, next to a concrete wall just a level down from the top. When the gunfire first sounded, Michael stopped next to an open slot: the space between the wall and level above it. A space full of zombies. Of course, the zombies heard the shots, and the screaming. *I* was screaming. Before Michael could even react, before the assholes on the ground could shoot him down, a dozen grasping hands lunged out from the garage and began to drag him in. He was still tangled in the ladder so they couldn't pull him away, but that didn't stop them from biting chunks out of whatever parts of him they could get to. He screamed, and then looked up at me.

"GO!" he shouted.

"No. No. NO!" I kept shaking my head, as if negation could stop everything from happening. "I won't leave you like this."

"Allie," he said, soft, but I could still hear him over the din of the carnage from the undead. "Go now, while you can still climb over me. If you wait, you'll fall, the horde will get you too, or the people below will shoot you off the ladder."

"More fingers clawed into his midsection and he shrieked, blood coming out of his mouth. The dead began yanking on him in earnest and the ladder was jumping around like crazy. I had to go. Somehow, I found my footing on the rungs below him and I passed over him, close as a lover. The last I saw of Michael, he looked down at me, his face white and shocked, blood staining his teeth crimson.

"Chivalry isn't dead, after all," he said.

Then he was gone, dragged into the garage. His screams chased me down the ladder. The ones who shot us, the slavers who killed everyone in the world that I knew met me at the bottom.

"There were five of them and they formed a circle around me. I was dazed, reeling, and scared to death. A strange combination of emotions. When I was a kid, my parents read me a book about rabbits. It was cool because it was so odd. The rabbits had a society, and wars, and bad guys, and a whole bunch of made-up words that had meaning that made sense to rabbits. I thought it was cool. What kid wouldn't like a story about kick-ass bunnies?

"The rabbits had a word, 'tharn'. It was what they used to describe the *in-the-headlights* fear, the kind that froze a deer — or in the book's case, a rabbit — in place, too scared to run or fight or even think. That's how I felt when I reached the bottom and saw those five leering faces standing over the bodies of my friends. Overwhelmed to the point where I was simply rooted to the ground, lost in grief and mindless in terror. They put a sack over my head and tossed me in the back of a pickup truck.

CHAPTER 10 -- CAPTIVITY

Everyone was quiet for a while. Even Sharon was at a loss. We waited her out, staring at nothing in particular while Allie worked up the courage to start again. She scrubbed a hand across her eyes and picked up her tale.

"I rode in the back of that truck, tied up, for a long time. The whole way, I could hear them whooping and laughing it up. They hollered back at me, gloating that there was nobody left alive who even remembered I existed. They told me they owned me and went into detail about all the shit they were going to do to me. Sex. Torture. Slave work. Then we got back to their place and . . . and . . . they made it happen."

Allie paused again, looking away from us, but she forged on.

"Th-th-the first three months were the hardest. I was a new toy for them and they passed me around between them, beat me and made me do, not just work around their place, but whatever weird humiliating shit they could think up. Bad enough if they'd been truly clever in their sadism.

"It was somehow worse that the guys were stupid.

"I swear, they didn't have a single brain between the five of them. To me, they were like the Three Stooges: Moe, Larry, Curly — plus Shemp and Curly Joe to boot. So, *Five* Stooges, I guess. All they had going for them was a shared kind of sick cruelty and their sheer physical strength. That's probably why they were slavers, they're too stupid to do anything else and too empty to care. Sadly, it was enough to keep me beaten down, both physically and psychologically, for a long time.

"In a way, I didn't get over being 'tharn' during that time. I went day to day, beating to beating, humiliation to humiliation . . . all of it, and worse. I just kinda checked out for a while. Even now, I can barely remember it. I just know that, by the third month, with no hope of rescue or end of the torture, I was ready to die. I went on that way for a long time.

"What saved me was that flat ignorance of the Stooges . . . and a loose section of chain link fence.

"Later — years, days, I couldn't keep it straight — they grew tired of using me as a slave and sex toy and, instead, began to just sort of neglect me. Sometimes, they'd forget I was locked in the closet they kept me in and wouldn't let me out for days. Other times, they'd force me to clean up after them in their pigsty of a house. Most of the time, they'd just ignore me until one of them needed something. Eventually, they even started taking me with them when they went out foraging. The first time was a surprise. I woke one morning when the door of my closet was thrown open and I was dragged me outside into the yard. For a moment, I thought they were going to kill me, but I just stood there feeling the dead grass between my toes.

"After so long locked up in their house, my first taste of fresh air left me feeling kinda weird. Almost giddy. That lasted right up until Moe tied a rope around my waist and they made me walk in front of them like I was a fuckin' dog. I guess as long as they'd held me prisoner, they thought I was going to be cowed enough not to cause them problems. Maybe I was . . . at first.

"We walked for what seemed like miles with the rope chafing my sides, or practically cutting me in half, whenever they decided to get cute and yank me back. We found a little strip mall in a long-abandoned neighborhood. There was a bar with busted-out windows. It was blackened inside, like it had been firebombed. The insurance office next door was fairly intact. The door was still closed, but through the window, we could see a couple of zombies standing slack-jawed and stupid. One of them saw us and mashed up against the window, trying to eat us through the glass. The second one seemed a bit slow. It didn't pay us much attention. For a second, the Stooges talked about sending me in to search the office for food or whatever, but they decided against it. I guess they didn't like the odds that the zombies might slip out and attack them. That it would happen after the zombies killed me didn't seem to bother them, of course. We worked our way around the buildings and tried a few stores and shops, which is to say, they shoved me in the front door and I had to hope I wasn't killed or bitten by something that might've been trapped inside since the world ended. On the backside of the mall, we hit a jackpot: a mom-and-pop pharmacy.

"Finding ways to get drunk or high was pretty hard, even right after society fell apart. Perhaps, *especially* after society fell apart. Looting cleaned out a surprisingly large swath of supplies, food, and other stuff, but it wiped booze and drugs almost entirely clean.

During my time with the Stooges, they occasionally found an odd bottle or six-pack of something — and when they did, they got hammered. Most of the time, though, they just bitched about wanting to get drunk or boasted about times they'd been stoned in the past. Finding an un-looted pharmacy? The Stooges were practically wetting themselves in anticipation of all the cool drugs inside, or more accurately, of my bringing back the good stuff.

"They sent me in alone — did I mention that they weren't very bright? They told me to get all the narcotics I could grab. It never occurred to them, as it occurred to me, that I could dump a bottle of Oxycontin and fill it with . . . well . . . anything, like laxative or poison. As it turned out, I didn't get the chance. I didn't know what would be deadly enough of a substitute to opioids to kill them quickly enough that they wouldn't catch on before they died. What I did, instead, was to grab a whole mess of heavy-duty sleep aids, then stuffed them in the bottom of a tampon box. Then I loaded up a shopping basket with all the "good stuff" I could find. I came out, waving bottle after bottle of narcotics. I even told them about the huge bottle of the super-strong stuff, the mixture given to terminal cancer patients to nuke their pain so they can die as peacefully as possible. I didn't mention how seriously fucked up they could get off that. Perhaps permanently. Live and learn for them, I guess. When they saw a basket full of heavy-duty drugs, the Stooges didn't even notice the bag of feminine hygiene products I was carrying. If they did, they didn't say anything about it.

"As we headed back, the Stooges were in a jovial mood, whooping and yelling and pushing each other around; talking about the 'par-tay' they were going to have that night. Idiotic, of course, making all that noise because when you whoop and holler around undead hordes, you tend to attract their attention. Before long, we were on the run. One of them, the Stooge I called Shemp, grabbed the basket of drugs from me. I don't think he trusted me not to drop it all or toss it aside. Maybe he just wanted to keep it for himself if everyone else got eaten. Who knows?

When the zombies started getting close, the Stooges panicked. They ran around the outside of a building (an old, cut-rate used car place), and huddled next to the chain link fence that circled the back lot, then stopped to argue about what to do next. They were so busy bickering that they forgot about me. I still had the rope tied around me and a good twenty or thirty feet of lead. For the first time since they caught me, I found a little hope.

"When they started *really* getting pissed and started yelling at each other — I did mention they were idiots, yes? — I scaled the chain link fence and dropped over onto the car lot side. My feet hit the ground and I took off running, as fast as I could. Stooge Larry happened to be holding my leash rope, he had it wrapped around his hand. He had only enough time to catch on to what I was doing and was just beginning to set his feet when the rope ran out of slack. It pulled up tight and I threw myself forward with all my weight to grab onto the bumper of the nearest car. My lunge yanked Larry right off his feet. He collided with Curly Joe, who fell into Shemp and knocked the basket out of his hand. Drugs flying every which way. Moe and regular Curly dove to the ground, trying to grab the spilled drugs.

"Then the horde rounded the corner. They were close. *Really* close. The Stooges all freaked out and started to run away . . . except I was still tethered to Larry. The moment they started running, I dug in, lunged forward again and yanked Larry off his feet once again. It was hilarious and liberating! I mean, I was very likely going to get eaten by the horde or beaten to death by the Stooges — assuming we somehow survived long enough — and all I could do was laugh. I couldn't stop.

"So, I'm almost doubled over, laughing, doing my deal-level best to keep Larry off his feet, while the rest of the Stooges were trying to get the rope unwrapped from Larry's hand, all with a big bunch of zombies bearing down on them. I almost got 'em all killed, it was that close. At the last second, they scrambled over the fence and got Larry unwrapped, and caught my rope before I could slip away from them. The pursuing horde crashed into the sections of chain link, and I was sure it would give way, but it held just long enough for them to regain what little composure they had before we left.

"We made it back to their place. I took the worst beating ever, and all I could think about was how funny Larry looked with me dragging him by his hand, using the tether they'd used to tie me, how slapstick silly the rest of them were. I realized then that I wasn't afraid of them anymore, even while they were knocking the shit out of me. I realized I didn't care what they did: they were stronger than me, there were more of them, and they could kill me anytime they wanted, but they were just kinda stupid and pathetic. So, I laughed at them until they beat me unconscious.

"From that point, things were different. I spent most of the next few weeks recuperating, locked in my closet. Eventually, they let me out, but it was another couple of months before they took me hunting for food again. The whole time, my attitude toward them was changing. Evolving. I started calling them by their Stooge names, but not all at once. I get the feeling that they never watched the Stooges because they never seemed to have caught on. I began playing them against each other, nothing serious, just the stupid kinds of things that people deal with when they're living together.

"I spent an entire month, for instance, playing around with leaving the toilet seat up or down just to see which of the Stooges paid attention when they pissed at night or sat down to take a crap during the day. Another time, I started swiping stuff out of one of the guys' rooms and hiding it in one of the other Stooges' secret stash. They damn near killed each other before I stopped out of fear they'd catch *me* at it.

"It was mainly little, petty stuff, but the Stooges had *never* fought with each other as much as they did when I was trying to get them irritated. Bit by bit, their happy home became somewhat less happy while my life became better (marginally so, at least).

"More important, all that time after the pharmacy raid, they never thought to check the tampon box I carried home that night, so I had a whole bunch of monster sleeping drugs, and the pieces of the vague plan I'd thought of that day finally began to come together. Given time, I might have even been able to escape once and for all . . . except the Stooges messed it all up. They came home one night, after leaving me locked up all day, and started talking. I don't believe they even gave me a thought, so it never occurred to them that I might be listening in. Even if it *did* occur to them, they would've never guessed the affect their conversation would have on me or what it might lead me to do.

"You see, the Stooges were excited, talking about this other group of people they'd found. Bunch of fools in a lumberyard who didn't keep regular lookouts and had relatively weak defenses. Moe got to talking about seeing a woman, while the Curly's and Shemp were practically drooling over the carnage they were going to get to see. Sick bastards. They spent the night, planning it all out. Something they'd obviously been working on while I was out of commission from their beating. A plan that had worked for them before, so they were going to try it again: throwing a herd at them, then waiting to pick off the ones they don't want while taking the one they did, the woman."

She paused to glance at Sharon. To her credit, Sharon had the decency to wince.

"It was pretty clear to me," Allie continued, "that they were shopping for a replacement slave. I mean, they *might* have wanted to add in slaves — the more, the merrier, right? — but I got the feeling that at some level, they realized they were having enough trouble controlling little ol' me. So, if their plan — their raid — was successful, I'm guessing I was going to be done for.

"It might've been a good plan for them. After all, it worked on my group at the parking garage. It could work again. They just didn't figure me into their equation. If they had, they'd never let me get close to their food.

"On my last night with them, I fixed soup. Soup is pretty good to have to feed a lot of people because you can cook up a lot of broth from a very little bit of meat. I made soup from a couple packages of beef jerky, an onion, and then all of the drugs I had. A bunch of codeine-based stuff, plus some stuff I didn't even bother to read what was on the label. I mixed a great pharmaceutical cocktail into their soup and then set it out on the table.

As usual, they served up first. And, as usual, they also ate almost all of the soup before I got my turn. Of course, I didn't want my turn. Not that night.

"I waited a half-hour after they crashed. I should've slit their throats while I had them all at my mercy. I don't really know why I didn't. I could tell you that I was scared one of them would wake up while I was cutting on him and make enough noise to stop me, or some such nonsense like that. I just didn't want to murder them in cold blood. I couldn't. It's a stupid thing, drawing a line like that, *not* slaughtering them while they were defenseless; especially with the world like it is today and especially after everything they did to me. I couldn't. I stood over Larry with the knife just an inch over his neck, watching his carotid throb with his heartbeat, and I couldn't kill him. I thought of the rape and the cruelty and the beating and, God help me, the knife dipped and drew a crease on his skin. Then I thought about how stupid he looked when I'd hopped the fence and used my leash to keep dragging him to the ground. I thought about the fear I saw in his face, the panic that he was about to be overrun and ripped apart. I realized I couldn't kill him, not in cold blood. The lazy fucker deserved to die, but if I cut his throat, what would I become?

"Instead, I left. Well, I left only after I locked all the doors and set their house on fire."

Allie paused for a moment, a crooked smile on her face. "I'm not *that* much of a saint."

We sat there, dumbfounded. Sharon broke the silence. "You set their house on fire."

"Yes."

"And yet, they're still alive and coming after us."

"Yes," Allie replied. "I stayed around to watch the place burn. Right before the fire really got rolling, one of the Stooges woke up. He woke up the rest of them and they all put the fire out. I don't know what I would've done if they'd stayed asleep. I hated myself, probably. I set the fire because I needed to slow them down and buy some time to come warn you. It might've been easier if I'd murdered them or made sure they burned to death, but I would still have to live with myself after. After all that time with them, I didn't want to turn into them."

"Do you think they're still coming?" I asked.

"They're coming. Especially since they lost me as their slave, but they were coming either way. They'll make their move."

"And we're supposed to trust you, why?" Stine asked. "After all, you've already lied to us."

"How did she lie?" It just slipped out of my mouth. I wasn't sure why I felt like defending her — or maybe I didn't want to admit it right then.

"She shows up here naked, like she just escaped," Stine said, "but she just told us she walked out of the house a free woman, with a gun, yet. We're supposed to believe she'd take a gun but not throw something on?"

I started to answer, but Allie held up a hand, the shadow of a smile playing across her lips.

"You're right," she said. "I left with a gun and my clothes, but not much else. I'm *not* lying about the Stooges. I was their slave. I did drug them and set their house on fire. Hell, I followed them for the last three days, watching them scope out your place here. When you come. When you go. They spent one of those days locating the nearest horde.

She passed her hand over her face.

"Look, I'm sorry I misled you. I just thought that if I came in here, fully dressed, with a story about slavers coming to force you out, you'd have tossed me out on my ear . . ."

"At the *very* least," muttered Stine.

"I thought that showing up naked would get me an open door, buy me enough time for you to hear my story."

"Well you got balls, lady," Sharon said. "And you got our attention enough to tell us what you wanted to tell us. But how do we trust you now?"

"You don't," Allie said. "I could show you where the Stooges live — or *lived* — but that by itself is no real proof that they're coming after you. I can't really prove it . . . until they come after you."

"So, what do you want?" asked Davies

"I want you to survive. With me, without me. I don't really care. Tie me up until they attack, but if you're going to leave me that way, do me a favor and kill me instead."

Stine started a slow clap. "Yeah, that sounds really good. It still doesn't make me trust you."

"*Don't* trust me," Allie replied. "It doesn't cost you much to prepare for the Stooges, whether I'm helping you or not. I'd just tell you to plan a way of getting out of here that's not your usual escape route, one where you can get away, even if the fence is surrounded and caving in from the weight of the horde. Be ready for them. We weren't, and I lost everything: people I knew and loved, a safe place to live. Don't let the Stooges take that from you."

Silence, then. Even Stine shut up. I don't know how long the moment lasted, but finally Carson spoke up. "I say we trust her. I say we get ready."

"And if she's working with them?" Sharon asked.

"We prepare for that, too," he replied. "She's right that it won't hurt us to be ready. If she'd been lying about working for them, wouldn't it have been easier for her to sit with them, let the horde force us out the back and pick us off one at a time? Why would she come in?"

"Do we need to vote on it?" Davies asked.

"No," Carson said. "I don't think it will hurt us at all to be on our guard. Time will tell."

"So, what's next?" Davies asked.

Carson smiled and said, "We get ready for visitors."

CHAPTER 11 -- STOOGES

We sat on the roof, watching Allie's Stooges. They attacked us two days after she arrived. Allie's warning that the Stooges were scoping us out ended up giving us a quick way of testing her. We left Allie inside and out of sight with Sharon, then the rest of us went out as if we were foraging. Most of us actually *went* foraging, but as soon as we were out of sight, Davies slipped away. He was good at moving around unseen, so he was our recon scout.

We went through a couple buildings — ones we knew were empty — just in case we were being followed. We split up and pretended to pick up a few odds and ends. After a couple hours, we came out of a building and met up with Davies. We headed back to the lumberyard and slipped in through the loose wrought iron spindle that we used as our back entrance.

Up in the loft, Davies told us what he'd seen.

"They're out there, the Stooges, just like Allie told us." He was careful not to favor too friendly a smile at her, not with Sharon watching. "I found all five, spread out around the perimeter. They're hiding fairly well. We wouldn't see them from inside here. Maybe if we were on one of the roof walkways."

"So, what do we do?" Stine asked.

"I think we need to be gone," I said, "but quietly, so they still think we're here."

Fortunately, we had a different way out. Under one of our buildings, there was a big floor drain that led into the storm sewers. We'd explored the route through the sewers around the time we built up the lumberyard and they became the hidden escape we could use to leave in a way that no one could watch. In a way, the sewer route made us luckier than Allie's people had been, at least. Her group had been caught by surprise, overwhelmed. Even their best plans weren't enough against treachery. Would an escape like the sewer have saved them? Maybe, maybe not. Given how quickly a surprise attack from a horde would hit, I think that even *with* the sewer we would've been sitting ducks without Allie. If she hadn't warned us, we could have been caught in the loft when the horde came through the fences and very likely wouldn't have had a prayer of making the sewer grate in time to escape that way.

Knowing what Allie told us almost certainly saved *some* of us, probably all of us. Everyone understood, perhaps even before Davies confirmed enough of Allie's story, that the Stooges were real and that they were watching us. Even Stine seemed to get it after a fashion, although he still went out of his way to act like an asshole toward her.

We began keeping a quiet lookout, watching for when the Stooges or the horde came, so they didn't catch us off guard. It was tricky, though. We couldn't flat-out leave without dealing with the Stooges first. We couldn't just slip through the sewer grate and run away to find a new home somewhere else. Even if we escaped tonight, these guys weren't going to just disappear. We lived in what used to be a big city, but post-apocalypse, it wasn't that big anymore. There just wasn't that much livable space for two antagonistic groups. *The town wasn't big enough for the both of us.*

Our plan, then, needed to take out the Stooges once and for all.

***

The slavers came the way Allie said they would: leading a veritable horde of zombies by taunting and shouting and honking the horn of their car. They were obviously going to try to flush us out, like they had with Allie's group. It might've been a good plan for them. It might even have worked . . . if we'd been at home when they got there. We weren't waiting *inside* the lumberyard. We were watching the lumberyard from atop a building half a block away. We picked our vantage point so we could see it all.

Just outside of our normal back exit from the lumberyard, we saw three of the Stooges. They were huddled down in stands of tall weeds, smoking and chatting as if they didn't care about whether or not anyone saw them. Then again, they thought we were inside and all they had to do was wait for the other two to show up, horde in tow, at the main gate at the front of the yard. From our spot, we could see the horde they were bringing in — literally *thousands* of undead — following their car. Even from where we were, we could hear them laying on the horn, drawing every zombie from within earshot. A glance back at the lurking Stooges, we could see them ducking down, getting ready.

Just before the Stooges' horde reached the front gate, Allie rolled up at the back. She was riding a motor scooter and was leading — get this — her own horde. Right on top of the lurking Stooges.

It was beautiful.

The Stooges in back had to have heard her coming. I don't know why they didn't do anything about it. She rode that scooter right through the middle of them and they just gaped at her, none of them having the sense to do anything but sit and stare.

***

Of course, we'd argued about this part of our plan: who was going to ride the scooter, what path could they take to avoid being shot, all of it and more. In the end, Allie volunteered and wouldn't let us talk her out of it.

"I don't *care* if it's dangerous!" she told us. "I'm not afraid of these assholes!"

"But it *is* dangerous," Carson said. "One bullet and they'd kill you. Or they could just knock you off the scooter and leave with you."

"That would not happen," she replied, her voice cold. "However it turns out, they'll *never* take me again."

After a pause, she said, "Besides, I *need* to finish it. Bad enough I couldn't find the nerve to kill them when I had the opportunity. I was a coward and pretended that burning their house would do the job. Now they're ruining your place and everything you've built here. It's the least I can do to make it up to you. If I'd just . . ."

"Stop," I said. "Just stop. Those guys would've come here, with or without you. They would've caught us completely unprepared if you hadn't figured out a way to warn us. You took a risk trusting us not to be the same kind of scum that they are, or worse. And still, you came here."

Allie looked at me, uncertainly, but it was Sharon who spoke up.

"Sure, you put us at risk, coming here. I didn't like you when you got here. Hell, I'm not sure I like you now. But all of us here have been together for a long time and if we've learned one thing, *anything*, it's how much it sucks to be alone. If you killed those guys, you'd have had no reason to come talk to us . . ."

"And no one else to go to," I finished. "You don't have to do this, ride the scooter and face those guys. Not alone. Not at all. Let one of us do it or come along with you."

"No," she said. "I'll do this. Let me say goodbye to them in my own way."

What could we do? We let her go.

Even using walkie-talkies to coordinate her timing, Allie's arrival couldn't have been more perfect. She rolled her scooter right between the befuddled Stooges, threw it down as she skidded it into the fence, and jumped to her feet, slipping in a single motion through the loose wrought iron picket. She was halfway across the lumberyard before any of them reacted more than to just stare after her. You could almost see the light bulbs popping on over their heads when it began to occur to them that something had happened. They just couldn't figure out what it meant.

Their curiosity about Allie saved them a quick death. As one, the Stooges rose and followed Allie's path to the fence. They were standing beside it when Allie's horde began pouring into the empty field behind them.

The looks on their faces was priceless. I grabbed a set of binoculars so I could watch them. I couldn't really make out what they were saying, but you could've run a soundtrack from an original Three Stooges short. I half-expected them to start slapping each other's faces or poking their eyes. Some silly shit like that.

The first of the dead almost caught them before they figured out they needed to get inside the fence. They made it in just as bodies began slamming into wrought iron, arms grasping between the spindles. A short pause took place where they looked at each other. Then, they turned toward the direction Allie had run.

"Uh oh . . ." Stine was standing behind me.

I swung my binoculars to track Allie. The plan was for her to run straight into the building where the sewer grate was, slip into the drain, and use a lighter to set fire to the pile of wood we'd left underneath. The whole structure was soaked in kerosene and creosote. Once the fire started, it'd go up like a torch and block that exit. She would've had time, but she slowed to watch. I think she expected them to get caught by the horde outside. Some of them, at least. We actually *did* plan for the Stooges to follow Allie inside. We just thought it'd take longer, giving her enough time to escape without them chasing her. We were wrong on that, especially with Allie's delay. She took off running again the moment they came through the fence, but they were still too close for comfort.

The Stooges rounded a corner and had a perfect line of sight on Allie. One of them yanked a handgun from a hip holster and started firing at her. The shots were wild, all over the place. The Stooges were running and shouting. Allie bolted through a door of the building with the grate, but a bullet caught her in the leg as she slipped inside. I could see a spray of blood on the doorframe.

"She's in trouble!" Davies said.

I heard, but I had already dropped the binoculars and was heading for the stairs.

"I'll get her!" I yelled over my shoulder.

The rest of them were yelling behind me, telling me to wait, but I was gone. Down the staircase, crashing through the door, I circled around our building and raced through the streets to where the sewer let out. I dropped in and ran. I kept running until I smelled kerosene and knew I was under the lumberyard, under the building where Allie was. I climbed up the ladder we'd left there for Allie, and shouldered the heavy grate up.

I didn't care if I got shot. I wasn't gonna leave Allie to the Stooges, their guns, or the flames.

I pulled myself up into the space above, only to find myself staring down the barrel of Allie's gun.

"Comin' for the barbecue, Brian?" she said with a grin.

"I . . . I couldn't let you . . . couldn't let . . ."

Suddenly, I didn't know what to say. I was out of breath, soaked in sweat and trembling, but not from exertion.

"Aw, Brian, don't do that," she told me, "No fear. Remember? I'm not afraid of these jerks anymore."

"I just didn't want to watch you die."

"Now that you're here, maybe I won't."

Allie turned and fired four quick shots at the door, which one of the Stooges had begun pushing open to peek inside. All I saw of him was an *oh shit!* look on his face before he backpedaled away. I don't think Allie hit him, but I figured they'd not be in a hurry to try the door again very soon. I was surprised that the muzzle-flash didn't light up the gas fumes, but maybe those kinds of things only happen in the movies.

She turned and grinned at me again. "Let's get out of here."

"This way, then."

I helped her down the ladder, then dragged the grate back over the opening. Below, I lit a saturated length of two-by-four, let it get going good, and tossed it on the pile. It roared to life with a whoosh of orange light chasing away the shadows. Then, I kicked the ladder into the flames, just in case.

We could already feel the heat of the flames, standing back as far as we were, and the air being drawn through the sewer to feed it. It wouldn't take the building above very long to catch fire. Heat rises and kerosene burns. The drum of creosote, when caught, would make it that much hotter. The building would burn, and the Stooges' only escape would be gone.

***

We watched Allie's Stooges, waiting for the inevitable.

Allie and I made it back in time to watch the last two Stooges, the ones leading their horde, scale the fence to get inside the lumberyard.

She wouldn't let me carry her up the stairs, but I still had to help her scale the steps. When we reached the roof, we were mobbed. Carson grabbed us both and gave us a big bear hug, grabbing Allie gently with his meaty left arm while practically strangling me with his right. Sharon gave her a hug while Davies punched me in the arm. Stine? He just nodded at her with a look as serious, and sincere, as I'd ever seen on his face.

I wanted to take care of Allie's leg right away, but she said we could dress it up later. She let me rinse it out with peroxide from our med kit, and then I wrapped up the bullet hole through her calf with a bunch of gauze. She said she wanted to watch, so I dragged a chair over by the others so she could have a view.

Inside the lumberyard, the Stooges were all together again, and they were all stranded. The horde at the front of the gate had completely engulfed the front side of the yard; the ones Allie had brought circled the back and filled up the burnt-out part of the original store. The blaze we'd started looked like a piece of the sun had landed in the center, choking black smoke that rose in a pillar above and filled the yard with a light haze. No escape from there, and we could tell the Stooges knew it. The stage was set for our floor show.

"Of the guys in there," Stine asked her, "Which one is which? I can't tell."

Allie gestured at a squat, bulldog of a guy, standing in the middle of the area, shouting at the others, who were resolutely ignoring him.

"That one there, is the guy I call Moe," she said.

Next, she pointed at two fat guys. Well, 'fat' was kind of a relative term these days, but they both had a bit of the Pillsbury doughboy look to them. They were working together to try to drag a long ladder to the fences — without much luck, I have to say. We padlocked them to a post, so the men were tugging madly on them to break a rung or the chain or something.

"Those two, of course, are Curly and Curly Joe."

On the other side of the property, a tall, skeleton-looking guy was pacing the back side of the fence, looking for a way out. Pacing in the other direction was an old guy: balding, gray hair.

Allie waved a hand at them and said, "The skinny dude is Shemp. Old guy's Larry."

"You call *those* Stooges?" I asked. "Your Larry and Shemp suck!"

Allie stuck her tongue out at me, but her eyes held mine for just a second longer than was strictly necessary. We lapsed into silence again, waiting for the inevitable end for the idiots in the lumberyard.

Whatever plans of escape the Stooges were hoping for, they weren't working. So far, the fences had held up for a good half-hour, but even from where we were watching, we could tell that they wouldn't last a lot longer. Neither the fences nor the Stooges. Panic set in on them, a little bit at a time, some quicker than others.

We could see it happening from where we were watching, as well.

Things got ugly after that.

Larry was at the main gate, rushing and yelling at the zombies, apparently to try to get 'em agitated or *more* agitated than they already were. Our best guess was that he was trying to get them to knock down the gate so he could circle around behind them and escape though the vacated gate opening. Yeah, right. As if the mob wasn't big enough to fill both the yard *and* the gate.

Panic. It'll kill you every time.

He'd rush the gate, so the mob there would surge and bend its frame, then race back at the last second. He'd been at it for several minutes, yelling and waving his arms around, but he kinda lost track of how close he was getting to them when he rushed in to yell. An outstretched hand snagged him by a handful of his shirt. Another hooked him by his belt loop or pocket. For a moment, we could see realization cross his face, and I swear he looked befuddled and resigned the exact way Wile E. Coyote's face looked in the instant before he plummeted to the canyon floor.

The zombie dragged Larry closer to the fence and more hands shot through to snag his ankle. Another zombie caught the hand Larry was using to desperately try to bat himself free.

"Aw dude," Carson said from behind me. "He's *so* fucked."

"Well," I said in a low voice. "The guy's a slaver. 'Bout time he got fucked for a change."

Allie shot me a look, then her eyes crinkled up at the corners.

Then she said, quietly at first, but with an unmistakable crescendo, "Laaarrrrryyy! Asshole! Come on dooowwwwwwwn! You're the next contestant on The Bite is Right!"

I just kinda gaped at her. We all did.

She shrugged, smiled, and then continued. "So, Larry, what's your bid on this lovely zombie showcase?"

At the fence, the deader who had Larry's hand took a bite that removed three fingers all the way to the knuckles. He yanked his hand, *sans* fingers, back, jumping away out of pure reflex. Hell, he might've even gotten away right then. Instead, he just stood there, staring at his missing fingers and shrieking like a little girl.

"Seems like a handy guy to have around." Allie added.

Sharon groaned, but did so with a grin. The rest of us kinda looked at each other and sprouted our own goofy smiles.

More hands shot through the fence and dragged Larry to it. The sound of his body clanging wrought iron spindles reached us, even where we were standing.

Stine chimed in next.

"Annnd our contestant, Larry, is up for Plinko!" he said.

Blood spouted from everywhere on Larry and still, he kept screaming.

"Oooh, I'm sorry, but you didn't win," Sharon said.

We watched Larry get torn to pieces.

"But enjoy our lovely parting gifts," I said. Earned me another punch in the arm from Davies, but it was worth it.

***

The other guys lasted only another ten minutes. With the smell of blood in the air, the rest of the zombies went nuts, crashing against the gate with frenzied fervor to get whatever piece of Larry they could find. The already-warped sections of fence were close to failing, but Larry's ploy at the gate finally worked. Bowing dangerously, it held for a second more, then collapsed with a shriek of tortured metal.

The undead poured into the lumberyard.

The remaining Stooges scattered like mercury dropped on a sidewalk.

The mob caught up to Moe and Curly Joe first. They found themselves in an all-out sprint from the swarming front gate zombies, which turned out to be an unimpressive display of speed. A regular slow-motion foot race.

Davies smirked, then began talking into his hand to make his voice sound like he was a cheesy radio announcer.

"*Late in the game folks, third down, fourteen to go. Ball is snapped and Curly Joe breaks through the line. Looks like they caught the defense flat-footed folks, cuz they're slow to react. This guy's flying! He's at the fifty, the forty-five, the forty...*"

"Are you kidding?" Carson said, a big toothy smile on his face. "Football? Really?"

In the yard, Curly Joe stumbled, briefly, but righted himself by snagging Moe's arm. Somehow, they both just barely slip past the clutches of their pursuers. As one, the men split and turned, streaking away in opposite directions.

Curly Joe cut left like a tailback — as if he was listening to Davies' play-by-play — and made a beeline for the fallen front gate. Undead were still pouring in, but we could see the gap they were shooting for. Both guys kicked in an extra gear and were starting to pull away . . .

Davies picked up his spiel again.

"*. . . Curly Joe's got the ball, but the pursuit is on his heels. Can he make it? He might make it. I think he's gonna break free!*"

Almost. He almost made it.

Sprinting hard, beefy Curley Joe still had a chance of bulling his way out through a gap. Then, just as he hit the opening, a new push of zombies crushed in. He disappeared into the mob, screaming in terror as they fell on him.

"*Oooohhhhh*!" Allie said. "*The quarterback is toast!*"

Big as he was, we never saw even a small part of Curly Joe again. And Allie rung up points with her *Die Hard* reference.

Moe, on the other hand, had cut right to circle away from the gate. If he'd kept his feet to continue his cut, he might have avoided Curly Joe's fate. Instead, he stumbled at the last second and fell into the waiting arms of the undead spreading out just inside the fence. Carson broke in with the obvious.

"Looks like they don't want no Moe," Carson said.

Watching as they swarmed in on the poor slob, Carson finished, "I was wrong. They got Moe, plenty Moe."

Shemp was near the back of the yard. He'd found a part of the fence that looked stable and was trying to use a couple two-by-fours to make a ramp to climb up. He got them placed between the fence pikes and miraculously made it up to the top rail of the fence.

What he intended to do from there, we weren't sure. It kinda looked like he was going to try to jump over the mob on the other side, or at least to clear as many as possible. Instead, his foot slipped, and as he fell, he didn't quite make the ground: one of the pikes impaled him. Ran it right the fuck through his hip.

We all winced, even Allie.

That didn't stop Sharon from chiming in, "Is this where I say we oughta 'throw another Shemp on the barbie'?"

"HA!" Stine covered his mouth, trying to look cool, as if he intended to laugh all along.

"No," I said. "This is where we say the guy was *Shemp-paled*."

They all groaned. I was inclined to agree. Pretty bad fucking humor. But somehow, it fit.

Of the lot of them, Shemp probably had it the worst. Stuck on the fence (so to speak) as if he couldn't decide which way he wanted to go, he was close enough for the zombies to tear at him, but not close enough for them to shred him as easily as the others. For a little while, they were just snatching bits of skin off his arms and legs. I think one of them was chewing on his foot. They eventually got a good hold of his arms and he came apart, the fence spike ripping through him, even as he screamed.

The last guy was Curly.

Somehow, he made it all the way to the roof of the one of the shelter houses. We'd made sure we knocked down our ramps, so he was truly on an island. He was Custer, making his last stand on Little Big Horn, and he was sorely outnumbered. *Deadskins* came to my mind, but even I wasn't asshole enough to be snarky *and* racist. Below him was an ocean of the undead. Instead of Custer, maybe he was more like Moses before he parted his Red Sea. He paced the perimeter of the roof, looking for a way out — for a chance that simply wasn't there.

Eventually, he gave up. We could see it in the change in his posture, shoulders slumped, head down. He went up to the peak. Walked to the edge.

Allie picked up again with the announcer's voice.

"*Well, Jim, as the East German diver prepares for his dive, you have to wonder if his heart is really in it...*"

The guy crossed himself — an oddly archaic motion, given the circumstances — and simply fell forward off the roof, like that scene from *Top Secret!* with the ceramic Nazi guard. He landed with a crunching thud into the dead below.

"*Oooh! Looks like he didn't quite stick the entry.*" Davies added in. "*That's gonna cost him points with the Russian judge.*"

We watched for another few minutes before filing quietly away. We had to get to our new place, we needed to treat Allie, get her on heavy antibiotics to keep her wound from going septic. Yet, all I could think of were ghastly jokes we made about people dying badly. Sometimes you gotta just laugh at all the bad shit that happens in your life, or in someone else's, apparently. I thought about Allie, and how she was beautiful and vulnerable and fierce, how she'd risked everything to come warn us when she could've been miles away and living on her own. I thought about the courage it would take to laugh at the people who had owned you, abused you, and treated you worse than an animal.

There's a lesson there, I suppose. A lesson that I would never have learned if I had lived out my life on my own. The years I had already spent living a solitary life taught me plenty about futility, but would I have ever considered the strength of laughter? Of hope?

I chanced a peek over my shoulder. The rest of the lumberyard was catching. A good part of that horde would go up in smoke.

"*Curly fries*!" I thought, shaking my head. "Why the hell didn't I think of *Curly fries*?"

CHAPTER 12 -- AFTER THE FIRE

We made it another year.

Another year before that ill-fated night in the overrun shack. If I was the superstitious type, I might've blamed Karma, the Revenge of the Stooges, or the Society for the Prevention of Stupid Fucking Humor. Really, though, I'm not the superstitious kind. It's just life. Life at the end of the world. It sucks, but what can you do?

We made good use of the year. After almost getting caught in the lumberyard, we took to moving around again. This time, instead of just aimlessly shuffling from hideout to hideout, we changed. From the very start, our group was probably one of the very strongest left in our part of the world. We'd survived over the years, but all along, we'd been missing something. Before Allie, life had become a trap: we kept busy with the business of living from day to day, but in doing so, we forgot about the actual living part.

After the lumberyard, we were different. It wasn't something that happened overnight. Lasting change never does. We didn't just automatically become happy and hopeful. More like... we started looking at life differently. Started having a little fun, if that doesn't sound too lame.

One time, Allie led us to a toy store. We spent an entire week playing stupid board games and building things out of Legos. Another time, Stine somehow dug up an old movie theater projector and stacks of movies. Whenever we got bored of doing other stuff, we'd all have a movie night, complete with decade-old microwave popcorn we cooked over a Sterno can. Of course, a lot of the movies Stine turned up with were pornos, but we didn't care. For a couple hours, we felt like normal people in a normal world again.

Allie and I kinda became a thing.

We definitely got closer. Friends, to be sure. Then something more than that. It was weird, watching how the rest of the group looked at us: the little sparkle in their eyes when they watched us walking together or holding hands. Except for Stine, who taunted us mercilessly about 'bumpin' uglies' or any other graphic sexual reference that popped into his scum-filled brain.

In truth, we didn't really go that way, not for a long time. Given her time with the Stooges, I was reluctant to push Allie before she was ready. She didn't seem in too much of a hurry, so I was just happy to wait. Happy just to be with her.

God, I sound like a sap!

Then again, I guess I kinda was. I guess *we* kinda were. When it finally happened, when we finally made love, it was wonderful, but that's not what I really want to talk about.

What I want to say, what happened in that year is that, slowly, bit by bit, Allie became our leader. She was our heart, for sure, but also our eyes on the future. On the horizon of what might be for us. It was something I could *never* have done for us. Not alone. I just wasn't built that way.

***

One day, Allie took us back to the lumberyard. She had a plan. It was risky. Even after the fire, we knew there were still a bunch of zombies milling about nearby. We weren't living very close to them, but we weren't very far, either. We needed to do something about them — something that didn't involve just shuffling them around to some other part of town.

We loaded an old pickup truck up with a huge plastic water tank like the farmers use. Only we filled the water tank with gasoline. We drove it to the lumberyard, a decent distance away, and tied the steering wheel so it wouldn't turn off from its general path into the zombies hanging around the front. Dropped a brick on the gas pedal, threw it in Drive, and let it go. At the same time, Stine lit the gas-soaked rag we'd jammed into the truck's gas tank.

It made it halfway into the horde before it got hung up, high-centered on something. Maybe crushed zombies. I sure hope so. The truck's tank went up with a *whoomp*, then the gas-filled water tank exploded, the concussion hitting us like a fist in the chest. The horde dissolved into light and fire. We stayed awhile to watch them burn, knowing that at least *this* horde wouldn't bother us again.

After that, we started seeking out other hordes to destroy. It wasn't like our 9-to-5, but we did it pretty regularly. It was cool. Nice to have a purpose again. A goal to work for.

Even now, I don't know if what we were doing was all that meaningful. Yeah, we killed a lot of zombies, but there are still jillions more left in the world. What I *do* know is that torching the zombies at the lumberyard made us feel pretty good. Made us feel better about ourselves. About our future. We even talked about searching out other survivors to try to organize a larger community.

Goals upon goals. Building people up again. Humanity's Last Stand.

Could we have done it? Could we have succeeded when everyone else we ever knew failed. When the entire human civilization failed?

Maybe. Who knows? We never got that far.

***

Thinking about it now, in my current situation, I guess it seems pretty stupid.

I'm stuck here, frozen in place in the backyard of some dead guy's house. Everyone else is gone. *Gone*! Our shack got overrun and my friends died and, as far as I know, the fucking zombies ate everyone else in the world.

Everyone. But not me.

More of the zombies in the yard are shuffling in my direction. I don't know if they can smell me or if they're playing out the odds — a zombie version of Blind Man's Bluff. What I *do* know is that there's getting to be quite a crowd in here.

Standing on the deck, wallowing in surprisingly powerful self-pity, a thought occurs to me. It wasn't really a lightning bolt of an epiphany that crashed into my brain right out of the blue. It was more like a shot from the ol' lizard brain, one that's just too fucking tired to care anymore. It was a thought, nonetheless. A whisper, really. The words of a lover, breathed softly into my ear.

Let it go.

Just like that, I see it: a path laid out before me. A choice I can make in a world with few choices left.

I can let it go. Let it all go. A decade and more of surviving the end of the world. Of losing everyone I know and everyone I care about over, over, and over again. Of finding hope and losing it again and again. Of fighting just to survive, but surviving . . . just because. Surviving out of habit, more than anything else. I can let go of hunger, fear, apathy, and mind-numbing boredom.

I can let go of loneliness. I can let go of despair.

All I have to do is move. Make a noise. Hell, for fun, I could do Peter Boyle's song and tap dance number from *Young Frankenstein* and maybe even make it to his "Puttin' on da Riiiiitzz!" line before the population of backyard zombies ripped me into even more pieces than they ripped Stine.

It wouldn't take too much. No way I could survive the loving attentions of the Backyard Undead Glee Club. But that's a feature, right? I wouldn't have to bear the burden of living like this anymore. I could let it go.

And yet . . . Allie.

Before Allie showed up, I was pretty much done. Futility is a mean motherfucker to fight off in the apocalypse. Why keep fighting, year after year?

What's the use?

What good is it, becoming the best survivor in the world, if the only benefit of your success is to outlast everyone you've ever known and everyone you ever *might* have known?

Allie didn't *do* futility. It just wasn't in her DNA. She didn't have time for it. Not when there were so many things to look forward to doing in the world.

Of course, she died. When I think about the blind stupidity in her senseless death, I find the temptation to quit is almost overwhelming. To simply let myself be killed. To let it go. The death that's available to me right now might not be painless, but it would be easy. Like pulling the pin on a grenade and dropping it on the ground: a few seconds of terrifying anxiety, a little bit of pain, and it'd be over. Except, of course in my case, the grenade is the yard full of undead.

Continuing to live on now would be so futile. Opting to die would be so easy.

Yet, I don't think that's who I am now. Not anymore. Not since Allie taught me that life is always worth living.

I take a quick step forward. The Sharon-thing turns, eyes latched on me like lasers.

"Hi!" I shout to the yard. "My name is Brian, and I'm an alcoholic!"

Sharon-thing was up the steps in a hurry, so I kick her in the chest and she launches back to fall in a tangle with the others zombies just arriving. I've got their attention, so I hop up on the deck railing.

"Oh, *boys*! Lookee what I got heyuh."

My Gene Wilder impersonation isn't very good, but for some reason, I've always been able to do Cleavon Little better.

"Hey, where are the white women at?"

I cringe a little bit, a mental face-palm. *That's my parting shot? Really?* Doing a racist line from *Blazing Saddles*? Here, at a time when racism is probably — finally, and for the first time — not a problem in our world? Yet still, it fit somehow. A stupid line, for a stupid day in a stupid world. Can there *really* be any better exit line?

Shaking my head, I step up to the top of the fence and balance precariously, hanging onto the eave of the roof next to me to keep from falling. On the other side of the fence, a knot of undead is waiting. They're only stacked up three or four deep. Beyond them, the side of the house is clear, all the way to the street.

Beyond that?

Well, hell, I don't know. There's really no way I *can* know. Besides, if I don't know, who's left to ask?

So why not enjoy the run?

I leap off the top of the fence, reveling in the irony of how Stooge Shemp died doing precisely the same thing. Unlike Shemp, I make it off the fence and to the ground. I land — if you can call crumpling forward and using my face to scoop a divot out of the grass, landing — and somehow make it up to my feet. I can't resist one last crack.

I call over my shoulder another Cleavon Little line, "And now, for my next impression ... Jesse Owens."

Then I sprint away, as fast as my feet will take me. I'm out of the front yard, across the sidewalk and into the street. I round the corner into un-scouted territory, giggling like a loon.

I don't know if I'll make it, running now into unknown territory, but it beats staying where I was. It beats leaving all hands-on deck, and *feet*. And . . .

Ah, well, you get the picture.

Sure, I could die. So what? At least I know that if I'm gonna go out, when I go out, I'm always going to take that last shot — my parting shot — before I take my final bow.

It's something my friend Allie taught me before she died. Maybe someday, I'll be able to find someone else I can teach it to, as well.

About your Author

Daniel L. Naden has always been a writer. It's an affliction, a blessing, a curse...a dominant part of his life for as long as he can remember. He has published work in the areas of politics, humor, philosopy, and of course, fiction. Dan's stories explore the irony in life, through the lens of horror, suspense, & sci-fi. His writing has appeared in great anthologies, like: **The Best of Horror Library: Volumes 1-5, The Horror Library: Volume 2, Dark Distortions: Volume 1**, and **Our Shadows Speak**, along with top-notch publications like **Dark Recesses Magazine**, **Vault IX, Astounding Tales**, **Ragged Edge**, and **Montage**. Dan's latest novella, **Parting Shot** is here - from **HellBound Books**. Dan lives with his wife in Olathe, Kansas.

Other HellBound Books Titles
Available at: www.hellboundbookspublishing.com

Dig Two Graves

In the blurred lines between good and evil - who will win?

Jezebel White is a court-appointed psychologist who runs an underground human trafficking empire.

In order to justify her nefarious actions to her conscience, she selects victims based solely upon whom she deems immoral.

Now, she finds herself being framed for a crime she had only intended to commit.

A detective has placed a target on Jezebel's back, and the time to catch her predator is quickly running out

Savages

An incredibly touching, yet unapologetically brutal trek through a post-apocalyptic wasteland of a civilization that once was.

Two strangers, reliant upon each other for survival face impossible odds, driven by little more than the primitive desire to live, are hunted by vicious hoardes of those who were once human - *savages...*

Mindless and murdering savages. Are they zombies? Are they still human? Whatever the other survivors have become, they no longer speak; they only kill and live like animals.

Parker and Marcus navigate through the ruins and battle through these lingering savages with no answers, searching for the last strain of humanity. Until one discovery changes everything...

The infant's cry shatters their already destroyed world. For Parker, the babe invokes the ghosts of her dead husband and sons. For Iraq war veteran Marcus, the child embodies his hope and gives him innocence to protect. For both, they struggle to determine if faded notions like romance can even still exist in this bleak, dying world.

In this grim post-apocalyptic portrait, the survivors face the horror of not knowing what happened to the world around them as they question whether humanity was ever human at all.

Puckered

Percy is kinky.
Percy is perverted.
Percy is a loner.
Percy is sneaky…

...But most of all, Percy wants to be left alone.

Whether it be a nagging mother or something from his past, it feels like he is always trying to escape something.
Will he be able to find his own peace, or will the real world catch up to him?
There will be blood.
There will be s**t.
There will be unusual sexual kinks.
But most of all, there will be murder…

The Big Book of Bootleg Horror 2

The second volume in HellBound Books' flagship horror anthology - this one bursting at the seams with even more fantastically dark horror from the cream of the rising stars in today's horror scene!

Featuring: Tracey A. Cross, Elizabeth Zemlicka, Shelby Thomas, Matthew Gillies,

Spinster Eskie, Stephen Clements, Ken Goldman, Nathan Robinson, K.M. Campbell, Cody Grady, Sebastian Bendix, Leo X. Robertson, David Owain Hughes, Timothy McGivney, Kane Gordon, Todd Sullivan, Mike Mayak, Edward Ahern, Rose Garnett, Jaap Boekestein, Brandy Delight, Stanley B. Webb, D. Norfolk, and Thomas Gunther.

Shopping List

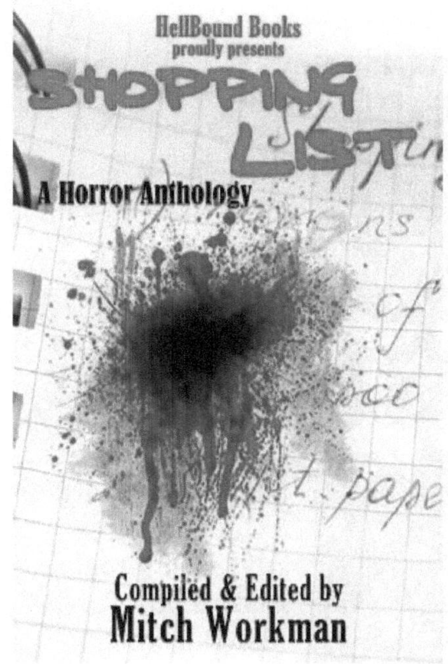

A simply superlative collection of spine-tingling horror from the very best minds in the business!

We decided upon the shopping list theme for this particular volume as an antithesis to those wildly successful writers (they know who they are) of whom it is often said *'we would read their damned shopping list if they published it!'*

Well, we have given twenty-one of the hottest authors in the independent horror scene the unique opportunity to have their own shopping lists read by you - along with their most terrifying tales of course!

Stories of gut-wrenching terror from:

Kathy Dinisi, Robert Over, Christopher O'Halloran, Eric W. Burgin, Russ Gartz, Mark Slada, Jeff Baker, Tim Miller, Nick Swain,JC Raye, Jovan Jones, Ben Stevens, David F. Gray, Brandon Cracraft, M.S. Swift, Kevin Holton, David Owain Hughes, Bertram Allan Mullin, Jeff C. Stevenson, Sebastian Crow and S.E. Rise

Demons, Devils and Denizens of Hell Vol, 2

The second volume in HellBound Books' outstanding horror anthology fair teems with tales of Hades' finest citizens – both resident and vacationing in our earthly realm… -

Compiled by the inimitable P. Mattern and featuring: Savannah Morgan, Andrew MacKay, Jaap Boekestein, James H Longmore, Stephanie Kelley, Ryan Woods, James Nichols, P. Mattern, Marcus Mattern, Gerri R Gray, and legion more…

A HellBound Books LLC
Publication

http://www.hellboundbookspublishing.com

Printed in the United States of America

Blood and Kisses

The definitive short story collecting from James H Longmore - an eclectic mix of dark horror, bizarro and Twilight-Zone style tales of the downright disturbing.

Welcome to the long awaited collection from the writer of horror novels *'Pede* and *Tenebrion*; a forword by Richard Chizmar (co-author of *Gwendy's Button Box* and author of *A Long December*), 18 short stories, 5 flash fiction and even a poem - all skin-crawling, soul-shredding tales of terror, of the darkest things that skulk amongst the night's inky shadows, and of the everyday gone horribly awry.

Discover the alternative implication of technology becoming self-aware, enjoy the acquaintance of a charismatic new pastor who promises his flock a brand new place in which to worship his God, and spend a little time in the company of a nice young man who is inexorably caught up in his home town's terrible secret. Then there is Cupid's revelation that personally he has never experienced love, yet we discover that very emotion alive and not so well amongst the ruins of a post zombie apocalypse world, and we bear witness to a childhood innocence forever destroyed in a war-torn city. There is more, Dear Reader, much, much more; for within these pages we have devils, demons and ghosts, lycanthropes and demi-gods, all rubbing nefarious shoulders with vilest of Hell's offspring who have slithered from the netherworld to doff their caps and wish us all the sweetest of dreams…

www.ingramcontent.com/pod-product-compliance
Lightning Source LLC
Chambersburg PA
CBHW051710180726
48283CB00004B/1287

* 9 7 8 1 9 4 8 3 1 8 3 1 0 *